"Kate Cooper, where have you been all my life?" Hugh asked

"Right here." Kate pulled her T-shirt over her head, tousling her short red curls. "Waiting to see what develops." She tossed the shirt away. "That's a photography joke."

"I like it." He liked more than the joke. He'd always thought black lace was the ultimate turn-on, but white lace had just become his favorite, especially when it cupped breasts as plump and inviting as Kate's.

She unsnapped her jeans and pushed them down over her hips. Then she paused and glanced at him. "Would you like me to take it a little slower?"

"Maybe later. Right now I just want all that stuff to disappear. I'm dying over here."

She smiled at him. "I know. When I was checking you out in the bathroom, you were looking...lumpy." She stepped out of her jeans.

"Lumpy." Not the most flattering way to describe his package.

"Lumpy is good." Then Kate reached behind her back, unfastened her bra and let it slide down her arms.

Hugh moaned in total appreciation. "No, honey—" he watched hungrily as she tossed the bra aside "—*that* is good."

Dear Reader,

One of the best things about writing a prequel for the COOPER'S CORNER continuity series is that it gave me a chance to go back to my Yankee roots. My family is originally from that area—in fact, my mother's family still owns a beach cottage on the Connecticut coast. And because everything in New England is so close to everything else, that cottage is only a hop, skip and a jump from Newport, Rhode Island, the lovely waterfront town where this story takes place. Hugh and Kate, my hero and heroine, sure have a terrific (and really hot) time there. I hope you will, too.

This book also gave me a chance to try something new—writing about twins. I've often wondered what it would be like to be a twin, and this story line gave me a chance to play with the possibilities. And finally, if all of this wasn't enough, I've had the pleasure of being tucked in between two of Temptation's finest—Kristine Rolofson, starting off the series with a bang, and Jill Shalvis, delivering the dynamic conclusion (at least until the COOPER'S CORNER continuity series starts up in August).

So spend some time in New England. You'll be glad you did.

Vicki Lewis Thompson

P.S. For information about my upcoming releases, visit my Web site at www.vickilewisthompson.com.

Books by Vicki Lewis Thompson

HARLEQUIN TEMPTATION
744—PURE TEMPTATION
780—THE COLORADO KID
788—BOONE'S BOUNTY
826—EVERY WOMAN'S FANTASY
853—THE NIGHTS BEFORE CHRISTMAS

HARLEQUIN BLAZE
1—NOTORIOUS
21—ACTING ON IMPULSE

Vicki Lewis Thompson
DOUBLE EXPOSURE

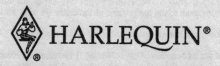

HARLEQUIN®

TORONTO • NEW YORK • LONDON
AMSTERDAM • PARIS • SYDNEY • HAMBURG
STOCKHOLM • ATHENS • TOKYO • MILAN • MADRID
PRAGUE • WARSAW • BUDAPEST • AUCKLAND

For Kylie Michelle Thompson.
Welcome to the world, little girl.
Your mommy can let you read this book
when you're older...say about thirty-five.

ISBN 0-373-25981-6

DOUBLE EXPOSURE

Copyright © 2002 by Harlequin Books S.A.

Vicki Lewis Thompson is acknowledged as the author of this
work.

_____Prologue_____

WHAT HE WOULDN'T GIVE for a hot tub and an even hotter woman.

Hugh Armstrong battled the frigid waves churned up by the studio's helicopter as he swam toward a perpetually sinking sailboat for the tenth time, a rescue line clenched between his teeth. The film's ambitious director obviously thought he was the next James Cameron and this shot of Antonio Banderas fighting through the water in the dark would win Oscars all around. Unfortunately it was Hugh doing the swimming, not Banderas.

People imagined the ocean off the coast of Southern California was warm and cozy. Maybe by August it would be, even at this time of night. But this was still June, and a cool June at that. Plus the chopper blades added a windchill factor Hugh didn't care to think about.

Normally he loved his job, but he had to admit his favorite stunts involved leaping from cliffs and crashing through windows. He was in this profession strictly for the adrenaline rush, and there was nothing scary about this current gig. Nobody would let him drown as he rescued the six actors on board the sailboat.

So instead of the stimulation he craved, he was stuck with boredom and exhaustion. On top of that, he really wanted to catch the eight o'clock plane out of LAX in the morning so he could get a jump start on his weekend in Rhode Island. Attending Stuart and Kim's wedding would be great, but the real draw was spending time with his twin brother Harry, who was Stuart's best man. It had been way too long between visits.

Plus he could use a few days off. He could *really* use a few days off. Another salty wave smacked him in the face, and he vowed this tenth take would be golden. Calling on his reserves, he put on a burst of speed that the director had to love. He made it to the partly submerged sailboat and secured the line quickly, determined that this time the director wouldn't yell *cut* as he had nine times before.

The cameras rolled. Hugh lifted his arms to the first passenger, an eight-year-old kid with a bright future in the film industry. The kid leaped into his arms, his fingernail gouging Hugh's forehead in the process. Hugh didn't even flinch as he grabbed the line and started hauling the kid back to the pitching yacht that was designated as the rescue boat. The cameras kept on rolling. Thank God. Maybe he'd make that plane, after all.

1

LATE AGAIN.

An old boyfriend had accused Kate of using habitual lateness to add drama to her life. She'd dumped the boyfriend in a fit of righteous indignation, but secretly she'd thought he'd nailed her motivation. Nothing got the adrenaline pumping like running fifteen minutes behind.

Heading out of Providence on the 95 toward the airport in Warwick, her Miata convertible's top down and the radio blaring, Kate cruised on that adrenaline rush. June marked the beginning of good convertible weather in Rhode Island, and she loved driving with the wind in her hair, weaving her little red car in and out of traffic, making every second count.

In no time she'd exited the interstate and was approaching the airport. She wasn't worried about successfully completing this afternoon's errand, anyway. She had a picture of Harry Armstrong in her purse, so if she missed him coming from the gate area, she'd nab him somewhere in the terminal. Hunting him down would be more exciting than standing around waiting for him to show up, anyway.

And look at that. A space near the terminal opened up like magic in the crowded parking lot. Kate whipped her car into the slot and switched off the ignition. Rummaging in her large purse, she found her comb, ran it through her short hair and checked her makeup in the rearview mirror.

After she dropped her comb back in her purse, she picked up her compact Nikon and made sure it was loaded. Taking glam photos in the studio paid the rent, but lately she'd had a thing for candid shots, from the hilarious to the highly dramatic. It was only a sideline—a hobby, really. She hadn't even shown her growing file of pictures to anyone. But these days she never went anywhere without a loaded camera.

After locking the car, she adjusted her wide purse strap across her chest and headed toward the pair of one-way streets separating the lot from the terminal. She'd always loved this airport. Inside the building, clearly visible through the windows, was a large sail-boat in dry dock, as if to announce to the world that this had been a seaport long before air travel was even invented.

She crossed the street at a jog, whisked through the automatic door and ran up the moving escalator, all the while keeping her eyes peeled for Harry. With regret she nixed the idea of grabbing a quick iced latte. Something about airports always made her want coffee.

As she searched the passengers streaming out of the gate area, she fantasized that she was a CIA operative on the lookout for a double agent who resembled Harry. Judging from his picture, he'd make a fine double agent—thick dark hair, square jaw and James Bond-blue eyes. Definitely a good choice for the best man in her sister Kim's wedding, especially considering that Kate was the maid of honor, so she'd be hanging out with Harry for the next few days. Still, she'd decided not to get her hopes up about him.

No doubt he'd turn out to be a typical urban male with a well-paying job, a late-model Volvo and a cell phone. A decent guy. Well, she craved excitement more than decency. Unfortunately, she couldn't seem to meet exciting men.

Men like her grandfather, for example. During World War II, Grandpa Charles left a wife and two young sons to enlist because he wanted to make the world a safer place for vulnerable young families like his. In a rain-drenched foxhole in France, he'd thrown himself on a grenade, sacrificing himself to save others. His incredible act of bravery gave Kate goose bumps.

Now that was the kind of man she wanted—except one that would not actually die. So far, nobody she knew personally had exhibited the sort of bravery modeled by Grandpa Charlie. She had little hope that Harry would, either.

Her mother, however, might decide Harry was Good Husband Material and try to matchmake. Now that Kim was getting married, the pressure would be on for Kate to do the same. After all, they were twins. A couple of days ago their mother had confessed her disappointment that Kate hadn't found anyone yet, because she'd always imagined a double wedding.

Kim and Kate had exchanged a twin-to-twin look that required no words. They'd both fought to keep from cracking up as they pictured their mother trying to dress them alike, one last time.

They hadn't been through that torture since their older brother Nick's eighth-grade graduation. After shredding those little green dresses with garden shears and threatening to do the same to any subsequent matching outfits, they'd been grounded for a month. But their mom had gotten the message.

Digging in her purse for the picture of Harry, Kate scanned the faces of the arriving passengers. She didn't really need to look at the picture again. She had a good eye for faces. Still, she glanced at it one more time.

He really was a cutie. She vaguely remembered he was some kind of doctor. Yes, definitely a doctor. Kim had said he and Stuart had gone through med school together. He was tall, Stuart had said—easy to spot in a crowd. Kate paused to study the crowd hurrying by. Then she saw him.

Damn, he was more of a hottie in the flesh than in the snapshot Stuart had given her. But the poor guy appeared to be exhausted. He wore jeans, a white T-shirt and a denim jacket, which made him look more like a rock star than a doctor.

The shadow of a beard covering his sculpted jaw indicated he'd had no time to shave before racing for the plane, and she wondered if he'd been at the hospital all night tending to a patient. That was pretty noble, come to think of it. Maybe Harry would fit her criteria better than she'd imagined.

He trudged through the terminal, a leather garment bag hanging from one broad shoulder by a wide carrying strap. When she hadn't been waiting to meet him, he'd probably assumed he'd have to take a taxi to the hotel. Remorse pricked her. Here she'd been playing tardiness games and he looked ready to drop.

"Over here, Harry!" she called, waving her arm in the air as she dodged through the throng to intercept him.

He didn't glance her way.

For a moment she wondered if she'd made a mistake. No, that was him for sure. Training in portrait photography had made her acutely aware of the arch of an eyebrow, the curve of a lip. That man was Harry. Maybe he was too tired to pay attention to his surroundings.

She should have been on time so that she could have met him as soon as he'd cleared security. But she'd make it up to him, poor man. She'd give him the VIP treatment for the rest of the day.

Stepping in front of him, she put a hand on his arm. The denim of his jacket was surprisingly soft. Expensive denim, she decided. "Sorry I'm late."

He looked startled, as if coming out of a daze.

Her conscience nagged her again for giving this guy additional grief and she smiled in apology. "I should have been here earlier. I'm Kate Cooper, Kim's twin sister. Stuart and Kim asked me to pick you up."

"Oh!" His expression cleared and he looked pleasantly surprised. "That's great. I didn't think anybody—"

"I know, and I feel terrible that I wasn't on time." Looking into those weary blue eyes, she just knew he'd been up all night. His voice was a little rusty, too. But it was a nice voice, a deep baritone that probably comforted his patients. She glanced at the garment bag. "Do you have more luggage?"

"Nope, this is it."

"Good. Then we can head straight to my car."

"Sounds good to me." He fell into step beside her.

"Stuart would have been here himself, except something important came up."

"I wouldn't doubt that. After all, the guy's getting married day after tomorrow."

"Well, that's exactly the trouble." She noticed that he'd matched his pace to hers and gave him points for that. Some tall guys took off with ground-eating strides that left her in the dust. So maybe he was considerate, besides being yummy to look at.

"Kim and Stuart are having trouble?" he asked.

"No, no, not that kind." Kate really liked the sound of his voice. "They just became a bit overwhelmed by all the commotion. My parents flew in from Florida, and my brother Nick came yesterday, and even my cousins Clint and Maureen arrived this morning. Stuart's mom is here with her new husband, and then Stuart's dad showed up with his new wife, and Stuart's two sisters have their hands full dealing with that. Anyway, there's all sorts of socializing and family intrigue, and Kim and Stuart weren't getting enough time alone with each other."

"Hmm."

Kate ushered him out of the terminal, and each of them paused to put on sunglasses. His wire-framed aviators made him look even more like a star on vacation than a doctor soon to be the best man in a wedding. So far this assignment of hers was beyond excellent. She could hardly wait to motor into Newport with this piece of eye candy in her passenger seat.

"My car's down this way," she said. "It's not far, but if you want to wait here I could bring it around."

"Do I look that feeble?"

She doubted there was a single feeble bone in his finely tuned body. Most MDs she'd met weren't this muscular. "No, but you look that tired."

His smile was wry, and adorably dimpled. "Well, I'm not *that* tired. Lead the way."

"Okay." Mmm. Great smile on this guy. "It's right down here. The red Miata."

"Sweet ride."

"I like it." Then she remembered how tall he was. "You might be a little cramped, though. Maybe I should have borrowed my cousin's—"

"Good grief. From the way you're worrying about me, I must look like something the cat dragged in."

If she had a cat, it could drag in a specimen like Harry any day of the week. "Not at all," she said, unlocking her trunk and shoving her suitcase aside. Not knowing what she'd be asked to transport down to Newport the next day, she'd decided to pack some clothes for herself and leave the suitcase at the inn where she'd be staying along with the rest of the wedding party.

That included Harry, of course, which was becoming an increasingly nice thought. "I'm guessing you haven't had much rest in the past twenty-four hours."

"You're right. I haven't." He swung the garment bag from his shoulder and settled it in the trunk with a sigh. "I wasn't even sure I'd make it here."

"Well, you did, and the good news is that you have tonight to rest up before things get going again tomorrow. Kim and Stuart took the ferry to Block Island and they're spending the night there by themselves to get their heads on straight before heading into the final stretch." She closed the trunk and glanced at him to find out how disappointed he was that he wouldn't be seeing Stuart right away.

He didn't look disappointed, just bone tired. He nodded. "That makes sense. Good for them."

Once he started toward the passenger side of the car, she walked around to the driver's side. "I'll take you to the inn, and you can just relax there for the evening. No need to get together with any of the family tonight. I think they all planned to go to an outdoor concert, anyway."

"Relaxing in a cozy inn sounds perfect."

Kate had already stashed her purse behind the seat and was ready to climb in when she saw a Great Dane sitting at the wheel of a Land Rover parked nearby. The dog looked for all the world as if it could simply turn the key and drive away. The window was down, probably because the owner knew nobody would try to steal the SUV with a huge dog in the front seat.

She had to have the shot. "Can you give me a second?" she asked Harry as she unzipped her purse and pulled out the camera.

"Sure, but—"

"I'll be right back." She walked over within range and snapped off a couple of frames. Then she moved to a different angle, shading her lens with her hand. Oh, this was terrific. She talked to the dog, who seemed to be posing for her by putting one hand on the wheel. She stepped closer. This was so wild, so totally—

The blare of the SUV's horn nearly made her drop the camera as she leaped backward. The darned dog must have slipped and put his paw on the horn. "Don't do that!" she said to the dog as she edged away, glancing around to see if anybody had noticed.

The dog continued to press the horn. As Kate backed toward her Miata, she began to suspect the dog was *trained* to honk the horn if anybody came too close. "Okay! I'm leaving!" she called to the dog. "Cut that out!"

Shoving her camera back in her purse, she jumped into the car.

Harry was laughing his head off.

"We're so outta here," she muttered, starting the car. "Who trains their dog to honk horns, anyway? Doesn't anybody use good old car alarms anymore?"

"Guess not," he said, grinning at her. "So, you're a photographer, like Kim?"

"Yep." She backed out and drove toward the exit.

"Freelance?"

"Technically I'm a studio photographer, like Kim. I handle the glamour shots and she's into kids and pets."

"What do you mean, *technically*?"

She hesitated, realizing she'd slipped up by qualifying her statement. When their dad had retired and left his two daughters in charge of the portrait studio he'd built into a fine business, they'd both been thrilled and honored. Kate was still thrilled and honored, except...except she wasn't having fun with the glamour shots anymore. Been there, done that. Taking the picture of the Great Dane, even with the horn-honking added in, had been fun.

"I guess I meant that's my main thing," she said. "But, I've started taking candid pictures for the heck of it."

"Where things aren't quite so predictable?"

"Right. But studio photography's rewarding, too. Very rewarding."

"I'm sure it is."

She had the oddest feeling that he understood her inner conflict perfectly, yet they barely knew each other. Intrigued by the thought, she glanced over at him. Damn, he was really shoe-horned into her car.

"Is the seat all the way back?" she asked.

He reached for the adjustment. "Uh-huh."

"Sorry the car's so small." She'd been so intent on driving her zippy little convertible on this warm June day that she hadn't stopped to think about how uncomfortable the car might be for a man who was at least six-three. Kim would have thought of that. Kim wasn't so focused on pizzazz, which was why she liked family photography so much.

"Kate, after what I've been through, it's minor."

"I'll get you to the inn as quick as I can." While they waited in a line of cars to get past the ticket booth, she switched off the radio. He might like to sleep on the way to Newport, if he could possibly sleep crammed into the seat like that.

As they reached the booth, Harry lifted up slightly from the seat and took his wallet from his hip pocket. "Let me get the parking fee."

"Absolutely not! It's bad enough that I was late picking you up." But in fumbling behind her seat for her purse, she nudged against his very solid body and discovered the close proximity made her breathless, and as uncoordinated as she'd ever been in her life. She should have taken the money out before she'd started the car. Kim would have done that.

The parking attendant cleared her throat.

While Kate was still twisted around digging in her purse for her wallet, Harry reached across her and handed a bill to the attendant.

"Thank you, sir." The attendant gave him his change.

Kate abandoned the struggle for her wallet and glanced over at him. "Thank you for paying, but you're making me feel extremely guilty. Let me buy you a drink sometime this weekend."

He smiled. "I'd like that."

She pulled away from the booth and slid the car smoothly into traffic, which was a small blessing. As jittery as she was feeling, she didn't trust her reaction time. The best man had quite a smile on him. Kim and Stuart had said he was a really nice guy. They hadn't said one word about him being a lady-killer.

That could be explained, of course. Stuart might not say something like that anyway, being a guy, and Kim was so crazy about Stuart she was likely oblivious to every other man on the planet. Still, Kate would have appreciated a warning from someone. The snapshot she'd carried to ID him didn't begin to capture his animal magnetism.

A more trained photographer—like her, for example—would have nailed it. She'd love to have a chance to try, but she doubted there'd be any time for a formal sitting. Still, she'd become pretty good at getting shots on the fly.

He leaned back, his neck supported by the headrest. "The sun feels great. Sure beats the heck out of swimming through cold water for six hours."

Kate did a mental double take. "Why were you doing that?"

"I had to pull six people out of a partially submerged sailboat. It took most of the night."

Her jaw dropped. "That's...incredible." It was more than incredible. Not only had he spent the night rescuing people from a shipwreck, he spoke about it as if it were all in a day's work. A chill ran down her spine. Had she finally found her hero?

"At least it went well. But the helicopter kept getting too low and churning up the water even worse, which made everything tougher. But hey, it's over. And I made it to Stuart and Kim's wedding, after all."

"I'm sure they're going to really, really appreciate that." A certified hero was going to be the best man at Kim's wedding. Hours ago he'd risked his life to save six people, and now he was riding in her car and would be spending the next four days in Providence. She could hardly believe this was happening, but she knew one thing for sure. She planned to make the most of this opportunity.

"I'm glad I could come," he said. "Now, if you don't mind, I'm going to close my eyes and relax for a little while. I tried to sleep on the plane, but my seatmate kept trying to have a conversation."

"I'll be quiet as a mouse." Kate was so glad she'd turned off the radio. Taking her foot off the gas, she allowed the car to ease back within the speed limit. She'd drive all the way to Newport in the right lane, letting cars whiz past her. No way was she taking a chance on jostling such precious cargo. "Just rest," she said to her hero. "I'll let you know when we get there."

HUGH ARMSTRONG closed his eyes and gave thanks for this little bit of heaven—riding under a warm sun while sitting next to the prettiest redhead he'd seen in quite a while. Since he was surrounded by glamour every day, that was saying something.

Maybe part of Kate's appeal was that she wasn't in the business. She wasn't trying to parlay her beauty into a starring role, so she could afford to be more casual about her traffic-stopping looks. Or maybe he'd been swept away by the animation on her face and she wasn't all that gorgeous.

Opening his eyes a fraction, he studied her again. Yeah, she was one-hundred-ten-percent babe. Probably used sunscreen to protect that flawless complexion, especially if she made a habit of driving with the top down. These days he couldn't tell if a woman's hair color was real, but in this case he'd guess that it was. She'd adopted the short, breezy style that was so popular, and she had just enough curl to turn those locks into tongues of flame whipped by the wind.

A white knit T-shirt, cropped at the waist, fit like a second skin. Hugh happened to love that look for obvious girl-watching reasons. Her hip-hugger jeans showed off a slice of midriff that made his mouth water. She wore open-toed mules. He couldn't see them now that her feet were tucked under the dash, but he remembered that her toenails matched her fingernails—both painted a wicked shade of red.

Five gold bracelets jingled on her right arm whenever she turned the wheel, and her hoop earrings were gold, too. She wore several rings, but her left ring finger was conspicuously bare. Good. Soon he'd find out whether or not she was in a relationship. If not, this could be one fine weekend. He closed his eyes again.

Usually he could sleep anywhere, but her sexy perfume kept him on the edge of wakefulness. She hadn't mentioned Harry. He wondered if sending Kate to the airport had been Harry's doing. Hugh had left a quick voice mail for Harry right before takeoff, not sure when his brother planned to leave Chicago.

Maybe Harry had picked up the voice mail and relayed Hugh's arrival time to the Coopers. He might even have suggested Kate for the pickup. Harry knew

Hugh's weakness for green-eyed redheads. So did Stuart, for that matter. They could easily have cooked this up together as a fun surprise.

Hugh thought Harry was supposed to get in today, too, but he could easily have been delayed. That happened a lot with him, because women never seemed to have their babies when they were supposed to.

Hugh understood that kind of topsy-turvy life. If the James Cameron wanna-be had decided the sequence wasn't good enough, Hugh would have been back in the water tonight getting wrinkled up like a prune again.

Instead he might be able to spend time with Kate Cooper, twin sister of the bride. He sure could use an in-room massage, though, and the inn might not offer that kind of service. He'd seriously overtaxed his muscles retrieving those folks from the boat, and he'd had no time to stretch and recover before heading to the airport. Five hours on a plane had left him stiff and sore.

That could cramp his style, and he wanted to be in top shape, just in case Kate happened to be available and willing to have fun this weekend. If Kim was even half as foxy as Kate, Stuart had done himself proud. Hugh was happy for him, if that's what Stuart wanted.

Personally, Hugh thought getting married was just asking for trouble. He'd once heard that creating a family meant providing hostages to fate. He couldn't agree more, and he didn't want to give fate that kind of power.

Worrying about a wife would be scary enough, but if he ever had kids, somebody might as well shoot him and get it over with. He'd be a mass of nerves if he ever had kids, considering all the dangers they faced these days.

No, he preferred staying free of those kinds of entanglements. Besides, he had a risky job, and he didn't think a wife and kids should have to live with the knowledge that he might not come home someday.

But the risk was all-important for him. For a few seconds after finishing a stunt, he felt invincible, and the addictive nature of that feeling kept him coming back for more and taking even greater chances. Because of that he was in demand. He'd done a few jobs others had refused.

That didn't mean he was foolhardy. He kept in shape, and he always expected to come through unscathed. But accidents happened. Timing wasn't always perfect. Everyone connected to a picture tried to be careful, but they all knew that the danger couldn't be eliminated. If it could, they'd let the stars perform the stunts themselves.

All in all, he loved his life. It was a glamorous world filled with excitement and beautiful women. Many of them sought the same brief, thrilling affairs that suited his lifestyle and personality. He wasn't sure about the rules back here in Rhode Island, but he meant to find out. He was free at the moment. If luck was with him, Kate might be, too.

2

KATE TURNED INTO THE parking area adjacent to Townsend House, the renovated Colonial inn that had opened a bare two weeks ago. Eagle-eyed Kim had spotted it when she and Kate were searching frantically for accommodations for the out-of-towners attending the wedding. By June most places were booked, but this place was not only available, it offered them grand opening discounts.

The wedding itself had been put together inside of a month, a speed that had left even Kate breathless. A few tongues had wagged, saying that anyone who got engaged in May and married in June must have *a reason,* nudge, nudge, wink, wink. Kate thought Stuart and Kim had the best reason of all for a speedy ceremony. They were crazy about each other and couldn't wait to make it official. Such reckless abandon was unusual for Kim, but it was exactly the kind of drama Kate loved.

Townsend House had started life as an inn back in 1702, and evidence existed that Benjamin Franklin had slept there. Now the building had been returned to its original grandeur, and its narrow clapboard siding gleamed with fresh white paint. Wedgwood blue shutters and window boxes filled with pansies satisfied both Kim's and Kate's finely tuned aesthetic sense. Rooms on the front of the house faced the harbor, while rooms on the back looked out on a flourishing rose garden and the luxurious honeymoon cottage.

Stuart and Kim weren't staying there after the wedding, however, not when such a gaggle of wedding guests would still be in the main house. Kate could understand the need for more privacy, but after touring the honeymoon cottage with Kim, she wondered if the newlyweds would find anything quite as gorgeous.

And speaking of gorgeous, Kate glanced over to check on her passenger. Still in dreamland. She shut off the motor and leaned toward him. He'd somehow managed to slouch down deeper into the seat, although he didn't look particularly comfortable. The fact that he'd fallen asleep squashed into the car testified to his exhaustion.

As a photographer she appreciated the classic structure of his high cheekbones, straight nose and firm jaw. As a woman she was drawn to his thick, dark lashes and sensuous mouth. She could have a field day with her camera, but taking pictures wasn't all she thought about when she looked at this man.

A sea breeze ruffled his hair and she noticed an angry red scratch on his forehead close to the hairline. No doubt that had happened last night during the rescue. He needed to put disinfectant on it. He might have other untended injuries, too. She would ask about that and make sure he took care of himself. Men like this often didn't bother about their own welfare. They were too self-sacrificing.

She needed to get him out of the car. Then she'd make sure he had something to eat, and after that she should probably leave him alone to sleep. Selfishly, she didn't want to do that. She wanted to hear more about his adventures. She had him to herself now, but tomorrow the dynamics would change and he'd belong to everyone.

"We're here," she said softly.

He opened his eyes. At first he seemed disoriented, but as the drowsiness cleared from those blue eyes, they took on a lazy, sexual warmth that curled her toes. With a soft groan, her superhero eased upright and unfastened his seat belt.

"Take it slow." Once again Kate wished she'd brought a bigger car. "You may be a little stiff from the ride."

"No problem," he said. "I've had sore muscles before." Nevertheless he grimaced in pain as he climbed out of the car. "Nothing a couple of shots of bourbon won't cure." His jaw tightened as he stood upright.

Kate popped the trunk open and exited her side. Then she couldn't help pausing to watch him take off his jacket and gingerly roll his broad shoulders. He had an amazingly toned body for someone who spent his days in the office or at the hospital. But now that his jacket was off she noticed a purple bruise on his left biceps and a long scratch on his right forearm.

Then she mentally smacked her forehead. She shouldn't be standing here admiring his body when he was in pain from his ordeal. "Let's get you checked in." She lifted her purse strap over her head and secured it across her chest. "I'm so glad you have tonight to recuperate before you get into the whole wedding deal." Then she opened the trunk and reached for his garment bag.

"Oh, no, you don't." He nudged her gently aside

and pulled the garment bag out of the trunk. "I can certainly carry my own luggage."

"I'm sure you can. I just think you need to relax." The brush of his body had set off quite a reaction within her. She hadn't responded to a man with this much enthusiasm since…never.

He smiled at her as he shouldered the bag. "I will." Then he glanced at the other small suitcase. "Are you taking this in?"

"Eventually. I'll have them store it for me until tomorrow. No need to mess with it now, though. I can come back and get it later." She started to close the trunk.

He put a hand on the trunk lid, holding it open. "Ah, let's take it now." He hefted the small suitcase. "For that matter, you can leave it in my room if you want."

She wasn't about to argue with an idea that would throw her into closer contact with him. "That would be great, if you don't mind." She led the way along a sidewalk leading to the inn's front door. Traffic on the street was heavy with people starting to search out a place to have dinner. She'd need to make sure he had a decent meal tonight.

Still, she didn't want to embarrass him by hovering. Naturally he would minimize the toll his heroics had taken on him, but a guy like him deserved lots of TLC. "Those six people from the sailboat, are they all okay?" she asked.

Tucking his jacket through the straps of his garmet bag, he walked beside her up to the front door, which had been painted a glossy black and accented with brass hinges, knob and knocker. "They were waterlogged and chilled, but yeah, I think they're fine. I worried about little Dustin, because he's only eight. He's a trouper though. Just grinned and drank his hot chocolate afterward."

"Amazing." To think that one of the people he'd rescued had been a child. Kate could only imagine how grateful the parents must be.

She opened the door into a hallway that was painted the same Wedgwood blue as the outside shutters, while the surrounding woodwork had been done in creamy white. The buffed oak flooring glowed in the soft light. Immediately to her left, a gilded oval mirror reflected a mixed bouquet of flowers sitting on an antique table that hugged the wall. Thank goodness she and Kim had been able to reserve rooms in such a classy place, fitting accommodations for a hero like Harry.

"But enough about that." He glanced around in obvious appreciation. "This is great. I want to forget about that whole ordeal and enjoy this weekend."

"All right. Check-in is over here." She stepped through a door on their right into a small sitting room. So he didn't want to discuss his rescue anymore, she thought as she rang the little brass bell that would bring someone to take care of the paperwork. Well, then she wouldn't mention the subject again. She could hardly blame him if he didn't want to relive such a nightmare.

But she wanted to make sure she understood his meaning. "So you'd rather I didn't mention anything of what you've been through to the others in the wedding party?"

He shrugged. "I just don't see the point. This weekend is supposed to be about Stuart and Kim, not me."

The sheer nobility of that sentiment made her weak

in the knees. Most men would welcome an audience so they could revel in the glory of their accomplishments, but this particular man didn't want his spectacular story to overshadow the wedding.

Then Kate realized something else. He'd trusted her with the tale, and now they shared a secret. She would be the only one at the wedding who would know that he was a bonafide hero. That was pretty darned cool.

"Okay," she said. "And may I say that's a wonderful attitude."

"Thanks, but I don't see it as anything spe—"

"It is," she said softly. "Now why don't you go over and relax on that sofa by the window and let me check you in?"

"Listen, I'm really fine. I can check myself in."

She put a hand on his arm, and her gold bangles jingled. "Yes, you could, but everything's all arranged, anyway, and it would be my pleasure." She looked into his eyes. "I promise not to bring up your ordeal again if you'll agree to let me pamper you a little."

His blue eyes warmed again as they had back in the car when he'd awakened. "A man would be a fool to turn down an offer like that."

HUGH DID AS HE WAS told and eased down upon a red and white patterned sofa just as a trim woman in a print blouse and khaki skirt came into the room and greeted them. Hugh stood up again.

"We're with the Cooper-Thorpe wedding party," Kate said. "I believe you have a room available for Mr. Armstrong."

"Certainly." The woman took her place behind an antique desk.

Kate glanced over at Hugh. "Just relax," she said, waving him back to the sofa. "I'll handle it."

Harry must have gotten his phone message, Hugh thought. Otherwise no one would have known to reserve him a room here. Oh, yeah, it was becoming very obvious that old Harry was trying to instigate a little romance between his brother and the maid of honor. The plan was almost too obvious, considering that Kate was totally Hugh's type.

Sitting down again, he used the time to study Kate. She wasn't very tall, only about five-five, but those snug capri-length jeans and high-heeled mules made her look taller. He had no idea how women maneuvered in those things or even how they kept them on. It was one of the sweet mysteries of life. However they managed to navigate in shoes with no back, some women had a flair for it, and Kate was one of those who could turn the whole exercise into poetry.

A multipaned window behind him looked out on the bustling harbor. He gave it a quick glance and hoped his room would have a different view. Boats and water didn't hold much appeal for him today, although he liked the idea of staying in this historic inn. Walking from the parking lot he'd smelled the saltwater tang of the bay and the aroma of fish being cooked in the area's restaurants. But in here, the dominant scent was of bread baking, which was more comforting to his battered body.

Still, he was happy to be here, harbor view and all. Visiting New England always reminded him of working on *The Patriot*, which brought good memories. He'd enjoyed getting to know Mel. And there had been a sexy member of the camera crew, Charise. He'd enjoyed getting to know her, too.

But Kate made him forget all about Charise, or any other woman he'd been with in recent memory. As he pretended to lounge casually on the wing-backed sofa, his thoughts were anything but casual. Kate had offered to pamper him. He wondered if that meant what he'd love it to mean.

In L.A. he'd know exactly what to expect after a woman made such an offer, especially when she had that special look in her eyes that he'd seen in Kate's. From the fit of her jeans to the daring neckline of her T-shirt, she radiated sexual confidence. Except for her height, she had the figure to be a runway model. Thank God that no longer described a woman with a flat-chested, boyish shape. He'd been delighted to see that trend disappear. Kate's breasts were perfect for the new, more womanly look.

She'd taken off her purse, one of those sling types that looked big enough to carry a small child, and propped it beside her on the floor. As she leaned over to sign the guest book, her cropped T-shirt rode up to reveal a strip of ivory skin. Hugh gazed at that tempting spot, focusing on the slight depression formed by the small of her back.

He had an almost uncontrollable urge to go over and rest his hand against her exposed skin. The heel of his hand would fit into that warm niche, while his fingers would curve around her waist. She would be soft to the touch, humming with energy.

He imagined her leaning into the pressure of his hand and turning her head to smile at him. His groin tightened. He'd have to control those thoughts, though, on the chance that he was misreading the signals she was giving him. Still, he couldn't believe that she looked at every guy the way she'd looked at him back there in the car.

There was the slight possibility that the atmosphere of the wedding had put her in a romantic mood. But if Harry had sent Kate on purpose, he would also have briefed her, letting her know that Hugh wasn't interested in anything serious.

Maybe Kate wasn't, either. Hugh had discovered that quite a few women in their twenties were focused on their careers and had no intention of tying themselves to a husband or even a steady boyfriend. He wouldn't be at all surprised to find that Kate felt that way, too.

From the way she'd talked about her photography, he guessed that she was dissatisfied with the status quo and wanted a change, even if she wasn't quite ready to admit that. Women in the midst of a career change weren't usually eager to settle down to a steady relationship. If she fit in that category, they were a perfect match for the weekend.

She finished signing the guest book and murmured something to the other woman that Hugh couldn't hear. The woman glanced over at him, so he could be fairly sure the conversation concerned him. Curious, he strained to hear what was being said, but noise filtering in from the busy street made it impossible.

The woman made a phone call, then another. Finally she shrugged and looked up at Kate with an air of regret. Whatever Kate had been trying to cook up, it hadn't worked.

There was more hushed conversation, and then Kate turned and came toward him, a key folder in one hand. "We tried to arrange for an in-room massage for you," she said. "But both recommended people were booked. If we were in Providence I'd have more of a selection, but I hate to take potluck."

He stood. "No problem. But it was a nice idea." A very nice idea. He was damned stiff, and a massage would have helped him be ready for...anything.

"I can upgrade you to a suite with a whirlpool," she said. "If you want it, that is. The only problem is that it's a little guest cottage out back instead of in the main building here, so there's no view of the harbor. No view at all, actually."

"To be honest, I didn't want to look at water and sailboats, anyway." And a whirlpool sounded like heaven to him. He wondered how big the whirlpool was, and if Kate...no, he was getting ahead of himself.

She gave him a secret smile and held out the key folder. "I had a feeling that would be fine with you, under the circumstances, so I went ahead and reserved it."

He took the key folder, but then he had a sudden thought. "I wouldn't be taking this away from Kim and Stuart, would I? I mean, this sounds like it could be the honeymoon cottage."

Kate laughed. "Kim and Stuart aren't about to stay here for their wedding night, if that's what you're saying. They love us all dearly, but they want to be far away from here that night. Even I don't know where they'll be staying, but I can guarantee it won't be at the Townsend House."

"Okay, then I'd love to have it."

"Good." Kate turned back to the woman at the desk. "We're all set."

The woman stood. "Would you like help with your luggage?"

"No, thanks." Hugh hoisted the garment bag to his

shoulder and grabbed Kate's suitcase. "Just point me in the right direction."

"I know how to get there," Kate said. "I'll show you."

That was exactly what he'd been hoping for.

KATE HAD TO RELY ON HER own judgment in this situation, but she felt certain that Stuart would want his best man to be comfortable, especially after what Harry had been through. And if Stuart didn't want to pay extra for the cottage, then she'd cover the cost. It wasn't so much. Well, okay, it was twice as much as a regular room, but the man needed some amenities.

Fortunately, this cozy hideaway had plenty. With a sense of anticipation she led him down the hall and through the cheerful breakfast room to a back door that opened onto the garden. The new owners had told Kim and Kate that they would have bought the property for the rose bushes alone. Although the inn had fallen into disrepair, the former occupants had been avid gardeners, and the dozens of blooming roses in shades of red, pink and peach testified to their skill.

Roses lined the flagstone walk and tumbled from trellises spaced around the garden. Water splashed in several stone fountains tucked in among the flowers. Kim and Stuart hadn't had time for engagement pictures, but last week Kate had talked them into letting her do some portraits here, and she was giving them the best of the lot, framed, as one of her wedding presents. The picture was so beautiful it brought tears to her eyes.

"Romantic."

She glanced over at Harry, and her tummy gave a little skitter of sensuality. "Yes, it is."

On the far side of the garden stood the cottage, which at one time had been a stable. But it bore no resemblance to one now. It had been painted white with blue trim to match the inn, and the effect was attractive, but the exterior gave no hint of the luxury within. Kate wanted to see the look on Harry's face when he opened the door.

He put the key in the lock and turned the brass knob, pushing the glossy black door open. As he stepped inside, he drew in a breath. "Ohmigod. This must cost a small fortune."

She smiled, pleased with his reaction. "Don't worry about it. They gave us a grand opening discount."

"Even so. I have to chip in for something like this."

Kate had to admit the place was spectacular. Set against a backdrop of mint-green walls, dark walnut furniture in the sitting area was upholstered in white brocade. Intricately patterned Oriental carpets rested on gleaming hardwood floors, and roses in delicate vases perched everywhere, perfuming the air with a heady fragrance.

Through a wide doorway stood a massive canopy bed dressed in the same white brocade as the furniture in the sitting room. And of course there were more roses. It was a perfect honeymoon cottage, Kate thought as she looked around. Or a lover's retreat....

"Beautiful." He turned full circle, his garment bag still over his shoulder, her suitcase in his other hand. Then he glanced at Kate. "Thank you." He hesitated. "Well, I've taken up a lot of your time. I'm sure you have things you need to do."

Maybe he was subtly trying to dismiss her. She

shouldn't make assumptions, even though she thought there was an attraction between them. "And you're probably ready for a nap."

"No, not really." He set down both suitcases and laid his jacket over a chair. "Maybe some time in the whirlpool, though."

"Then I should be going." She didn't want to leave, but she couldn't very well hang around while he took a long soak.

"So you *do* have things to take care of." His gaze was clearly regretful.

"Nothing earth-shattering, but I thought—"

"For all I know some guy's tapping his foot, wondering when you're going to show up for dinner."

Her pulse rate moved up a notch. He wanted to know if she had a boyfriend. "No," she said carefully. "Nobody's waiting for me." She looked into his eyes. "But maybe you need to call someone to let her know you arrived safely?"

He held her gaze as he shook his head.

"Oh." Her pulse raced at the unspoken messages zinging back and forth.

"I can hold off on the whirlpool, if you're free for dinner."

"I'm free for dinner, but I think you need to do something for those stiff muscles."

He shrugged. "I will, eventually." Then he gestured toward the suitcases. "Let me put these away."

"Okay." She waited in the sitting room while he carried both suitcases into the bedroom. Wow. This was turning into a fantasy event.

After he'd disappeared from view, a low whistle of appreciation filtered back to her. "Some whirlpool."

She remembered it well. Set into a bay window, the

marble tub was big enough for at least two people. By day the windows looked out on more rose bushes. By night, translucent shades provided complete privacy.

"And I look like a street person," he added.

"You look fine," she called to him. More than fine. Awesome. Hot.

"I need a shave." He came back out, rolling his shoulders. "Have you seen that whirlpool?"

She nodded. "Kim and I had the full tour when we booked the rooms for the wedding party." Watching him work the kinks from his shoulders made her long to go over and massage those knots out for him. That's what he really needed. A whirlpool wouldn't necessarily help his neck and shoulders.

"Well, I can tell you one thing. Before I take you out to dinner, I'm going to shave and clean up a little."

"You don't have to go to all that trouble. We can just—"

"Nope, I'll feel a lot better if I do. Give me five minutes."

"That's silly." The last thing she wanted to do was create more complications for him. "Listen, there's a submarine sandwich place a block away. I'll go pick up some food and bring it back. That way you can stay and relax."

"Look, I'm really fine. A quick shave and shower and I'll be good to go."

"You don't like subs?"

"I love them."

"Then it's settled." She started for the door. This evening was becoming more exciting by the minute. Now they'd be able to have their meal in total privacy. "What kind of sandwich do you want?"

"I eat anything. Surprise me."

She gave him a quick grin. "That's what I like, a man with a sense of adventure."

He smiled back. "Then I'm your guy."

3

KATE DECIDED THAT WALKING to the sub shop would be faster than trying to maneuver her car through the dense traffic, not to mention the challenge of finding a parking spot once she got there. She set out at a brisk pace, enjoying the salty air and the cry of the seagulls overhead. Walking also gave her a chance to consider the idea that had lodged in her brain and wouldn't leave.

Harry needed a massage. She had a basic knowledge of massage techniques. They'd have to work with the bed instead of using a massage table, but she'd had a little practice at that. She was no professional, but she was better than nothing. Besides, she'd had a massage nearly every week for the past five years, and then there was the crash course she and her ex-boyfriend Jonathan had taken last summer.

Although Jonathan hadn't thrived in that class, she'd had a great time. Come to think of it, his lack of interest in the massage class had marked the beginning of the end, although she'd never thought Jonathan was the answer to her prayers in the first place.

But Harry...Harry had definite possibilities. She had only one quibble. A stupid and superficial quibble it was, too, and she was a little ashamed of herself. She wished he had a different name. A guy named Harry would be the kind who remembered to take out the garbage and put air in the tires, a nice enough fellow, but not the sort she'd associate with grand passion and undying love.

Yet everything else about this man seemed totally perfect. Maybe she'd avoid using his name for the time being, and if everything worked out between them she'd create her own special name for him later on. Maybe he had a great middle name she could convince him to use.

After reaching the sub shop, she had to stand in line for a few minutes before placing her order for two eight-inchers, one hot pastrami and one Italian meatball, and a couple of large Cokes. The twenty-minute wait for the order gave her enough time to run back to the combination souvenir shop and drugstore that she'd noticed on the way here. If she couldn't find what she needed there, she'd take it as a sign that she was on the wrong track with this massage plan.

Inside the store, she stood and surveyed the display of T-shirts, miniature lighthouses and shell jewelry. The place was crowded, like everywhere else in Newport on this June evening. She glanced at her watch and waited with more than a little impatience for browsers to move out of the way so she could continue her search. She'd never meandered in her life, and it made her crazy when confronted with such a random waste of time.

Just when she was about to give up, the woman blocking a particular glass shelving unit walked to the far side of the shop. Sure enough, the top shelf held a set of three scented oils. Kate only needed the bottle of almond, but she didn't mind paying for the other two.

As she took the shrink-wrapped basket containing the oils to the front of the store and handed them to the woman standing at the register, she glanced behind the counter and noticed a tube of antiseptic cream. That would be good for the cut on Harry's forehead. Kate asked the clerk to add that to her purchase.

Then another item on the rack behind the counter caught Kate's eye. She didn't usually keep such an item with her, yet, under the circumstances, it might become essential. Still, buying it in advance seemed...weird. Of course, she considered herself a sexually liberated woman, so it shouldn't seem weird. Yet she'd never bought this particular item before.

"Will that be all?" the dark-haired woman asked with a smile.

"Um...." Kate hesitated as she quickly reviewed the situation. She was about to give Harry a massage, assuming he agreed to that. She thought he would. Secondly, he was attracted to her, or else he wouldn't have been fishing around trying to find out if she had a boyfriend.

If that attraction led to something more, she was open to that possibility. Yes, it was all happening fast, but Harry wasn't some stranger she'd picked up in a bar. He was Stuart's best friend, a respected medical professional, and a certified hero. He'd only be in Rhode Island for the weekend, so she didn't have a lot of time to play the dating game. And she was dying to be swept away.

Yet she was unprepared in one very important way to be swept away, and she had to assume he was, too. Now was her chance to remedy that, if she had the nerve. Was she willing to lose a golden opportunity out of a stupid sense of false modesty? So what if she was buying massage oil at the same time?

The clerk waited expectantly.

Kate took a deep breath. Nothing ventured, nothing gained. "I'll take a package of those." She pointed toward the display.

The clerk turned toward the back wall. "Which package?" she asked.

"The...the red one."

The clerk pulled the package from the display and laid it on the counter next to the basket of massage oil and antiseptic cream while she rang up all three purchases. The array was pretty damned suggestive, and Kate willed the clerk to proceed a little faster.

Of course the woman fumbled, hit the wrong keys, had to void out the tape and start over. Kate drummed her fingers on the counter and stared into space with as much sophisticated nonchalance as she could muster. But when the clerk finished ringing up the items and started to put everything in one bag, Kate stopped her.

"I'll take those in my purse," she said, snatching the condoms. With all the stuff already crammed in there, she had a devil of a time working the package to the bottom. Her bracelets jangled as she pulled out her wallet and moved aside her camera, compact, lipstick, lip pencil, mascara, blush, a pad of paper, two spare rolls of film, an emery board, a packet of tissues, breath mints and three ballpoint pens.

"Do you want your receipt in the bag?" asked the clerk.

"Yes. I mean, no, I'll just take it." Kate grabbed the receipt and stuffed it in her wallet the minute she realized that it probably spelled out exactly what she'd bought besides massage oil. She didn't have the nerve to look at the clerk again as she snapped her wallet shut, crammed it into her purse and whisked the plastic bag containing the oil off the counter.

Ten minutes later she'd picked up the food order and was on her way back to the inn. The closer she came, the faster her heart beat. She'd complained in the past about the lack of excitement in her life. Now here she was faced with the possibility of genuine, twenty-four-carat excitement, and she was scared. For one thing, she might be rejected. For another, she might not.

But this was what she'd longed for ever since she'd read *Gone With the Wind* at the age of eleven. Time to put up or shut up. Taking a deep breath, she walked into the Townsend House and down the hall toward the back door that led into the rose garden. She wondered if Harry had shaved.

FIRST HUGH UNPACKED. Then, when Kate still hadn't returned, he unzipped his shaving kit, stripped off his T-shirt and lathered up his day-old beard. As he stroked the razor through the minty foam, he started going over his pre-relationship ritual, the trick he'd used for years to keep himself from getting in too deep with a woman. He figured that most men ended up seriously involved with someone because they focused on all her good traits and ignored her flaws.

Hugh took time to appreciate a woman's good qualities, but he searched for at least one flaw to keep him from going overboard and falling in love. Whenever he felt his objectivity slipping, he concentrated on that flaw until he no longer had the urge to spend the rest of his life with the current object of his affection.

He wasn't shy about announcing his own shortcomings, either, so that the women in his life could take the same preventative measures. He wasn't wild about cocktail parties and he didn't like board games. He wasn't much for cards, either, and if someone suggested playing charades, he'd been known to vacate the premises.

Even worse as far as some women were concerned, he had a lousy memory for special occasions. He liked giving gifts but they didn't necessarily arrive on the appropriate day. But his biggest fault, at least for most of the women he'd dated, was his refusal to fall in love with them or talk about the possibility of commitment. He wasn't into that, but a few had thought they could change his mind.

He understood where they were coming from. The atmosphere in Hollywood encouraged falling in love—not so much with a person as with the fantasy image that person projected. His friends were always doing it, from megabuck stars to bit players. Then they inevitably discovered the person behind the fantasy and fell out of love again.

If Hugh was convinced he'd fall out of love, he might risk it. His real fear was that once he let down his guard he'd end up in so deep he'd never get out. Whenever Kate smiled at him, that fear took him by the throat. He needed to discover a flaw in her, and he needed to discover it fast.

Unfortunately he didn't have anything against photographers. He'd always admired the profession, because without it those who worked in front of the cameras wouldn't have a job. He also liked the restless spirit that was driving her to build a portfolio of candid shots. Even if she wouldn't admit it, she was ready to leave the confines of studio photography for a less controlled atmosphere.

He'd love to see her latest work. With some of his connections in L.A., he might be able to...whoa, bad sign. One of the safe things about Kate was her location, clear across the country from him. He definitely should not be dreaming up ways that she could eliminate that comfortable distance between them by landing some photo assignments in L.A.

No, he needed to find something wrong with her, and all he could see were her good points. She had such energy. He didn't often find someone with energy to match his own.

Of course, she didn't know he could match her energy, because at the moment he was operating at a low-battery level. If he'd known she was waiting for him at the end of the plane trip, he would have found a way to tune out the motormouth who'd sat next to him and kept him awake the whole flight.

No doubt about it, Kate was terrific. He'd become fascinated with the way her short hair created swirls of bright color each time she moved her head. Until this moment he hadn't cared much for short hair on a woman, but it suited Kate perfectly. He wanted to run his fingers through all that riot of color—tongues of fire he'd love to burn his hands on.

And speaking of tongues, she had an adorable habit of sliding the pink tip of hers along her upper lip and tilting her head to gaze at him, which made her look both mischievous and sexy as hell.

He grabbed a towel to dry his face just as a sharp knock came at the door to the cottage. Grinning, he walked to the entrance. No timid little tapping for Kate Cooper. "Who is it?" he called out.

"Room service," she called back, sassy as can be.

He swung open the door. "Took you long enough."

She breezed in, bringing with her the aroma of hot marinara sauce. "You might as well know the worst thing about me."

Good. She was going to announce a flaw, which he desperately needed to hear about. "What's that?"

Her gaze flicked over his bare chest and her cheeks turned pink.

He hadn't meant to be provocative, but her blush indicated that his semi-nudity was affecting her. "I'll go get a shirt," he said.

"No, that's okay," she said quickly, too quickly.

"I meant to put one on, but when you knocked, I—"

"Seriously, don't worry about it." She took a quick breath. "In fact, I thought after we finished eating I'd give you a massage."

His pulse quickened. "You did?"

Her cheeks grew even pinker, but she rushed bravely on. "That's the best thing for your neck and shoulders, better than the hot tub, and I have some training, plus I've had a whole bunch of massages myself, so I think I could do a good job."

"You don't have to convince me." He was overjoyed. One particular part of his body was extremely overjoyed, and he'd have to work on keeping that bad boy under control. "I'd love it."

"Great. Then let's eat." She put her other paper sack on the floor and began unpacking the sandwiches and drinks from the first one.

He had a sudden attack of remorse. "I didn't give you any money for this."

"I didn't expect you to." She motioned him to a chair. "Have a seat. I have hot pastrami and hot Italian meatball. You can have either, or some of both, or—"

"Some of both, and I want to pay for this. I invited

you to dinner, remember?" He must really be tired to have forgotten the money thing.

She shook her head. "This is my treat, considering that I was so late picking you up. That's what I started to tell you, the really bad thing about me." She divided each sandwich expertly in half before pushing the wrapper containing his portion towards him.

He needed to hear this fatal flaw of hers. Later he'd figure out what to do about picking up the tab for this meal. Sitting down, he glanced across the table. "So what about you is so terrible?" He hoped it would be atrocious.

Before sitting down, she gave each of them a soft drink and a straw. "The main thing that drives Kim and my friends nuts is that I tend to run late most of the time." She jammed her straw through the cup's plastic lid. "It's a bad habit that I can't seem to break. I try to cram too much into my schedule. That's why I was late coming to the airport. And I made a detour while I was getting the sandwiches, so that took longer than it should have, too."

"You weren't *that* late." Damn. Lateness wasn't a particular problem for him. He'd spent a great deal of time hanging around the set waiting for this actor or that one to show up, or for the director to arrive, or for the animals to do the stunts they were trained to do. He'd learned early that in order to stay sane he had to become patient and forget about the clock.

"Try having it happen all the time. You'd get irritated." She bit into her sandwich.

"Maybe so." He started in on his sandwich, too. He wished he could buy into this lateness problem of hers, but as a fatal flaw, it lacked punch. He was too good at coping.

"Kim's threatened me with bodily harm if I'm late to the wedding, but I've promised her I won't be. I mean, that's too important to mess around."

"Right." He couldn't take his eyes off her. She was becoming damned near irresistible, and that wasn't good.

"It'll be a wonderful wedding. I don't know if you've ever heard of the Newport mansions."

He shook his head.

"They date back to the Gilded Age, when people like the Rockefellers and John Jacob Astor had homes here. We lucked out, because a bride who'd booked Belcourt Castle two years ago canceled at the last minute. We not only got it, but they gave us a deal." She used her hands when she talked, which made her bracelets tinkle merrily.

She was so animated, so appealing, so downright sexy. He could sit and listen to her all night. Well, maybe not. Eventually he'd have to heed the call to action that was making his groin tighten and his pulse rate climb. "Sounds as if everything fell into place for Stuart and Kim," he said.

She laughed. "Once they figured out they were meant for each other, it did. Before that, it was rough going."

He'd never believed that people were meant for each other. If he had, he might be in more trouble than he already was.

As she described Kim and Stuart's rocky courtship, he kept searching for that deal-breaking flaw. Sometimes he discovered that a woman's voice grated on his ears, but Kate's was low-pitched and melodious. He could imagine that in some situations her voice would be soothing. This was not that kind of situation.

The sound of her voice made him think of cool sheets and warm bodies.

And with that voice she'd offered to give him a massage. She made it sound like a neighborly gesture, but he didn't think it would end up that way. Before he agreed to this massage, he needed to have his game plan. At the moment, he had none, and they were finished with their meal.

She balled up her sandwich wrapper and tossed it in the bag with a jingle of bracelets. "Well, I guess we should get started on that massage." The color in her cheeks deepened.

"I guess so." A surge of adrenaline caught him by surprise. He usually felt this way before performing a particularly difficult stunt. He couldn't remember ever feeling that way the moment he was alone with a woman. His chest was tight with anticipation.

She rattled the ice in her cup. "Are you finished with your Coke? I didn't mean to rush you."

"I'm finished. The sandwiches were great. Thanks again." He crumpled his wrapper and aimed a shot at the open bag. Ordinarily he would have sunk the basket, no problem. He missed.

"Air ball." With a smile, she retrieved the crumpled wrapper and tucked it in the bag.

"I must not have my head in the game."

"I'm sure you don't. You've been through a lot. I promised not to talk about it anymore, but that doesn't mean I've forgotten." She leaned down and pulled a small box from the second bag she'd brought in. "I bought a tube of antiseptic ointment, too. I want to put that on your scratches. Are there any others besides the one on your forehead and the one on your arm?"

"I don't think so." He'd forgotten all about the scratches. Having her notice them and go to the trouble and expense of getting something to put on them touched him. He wasn't used to having someone fuss over him. Correction—he'd never wanted anyone to fuss over him. He'd gone to great lengths to make sure everyone he worked with thought of him as indestructible and oblivious to pain.

Because Kate wasn't part of that world she didn't know the drill. And come to find out, he liked knowing she was concerned about his minor injuries. Besides, he could allow her to tend his wounds because no one would know about it and his image as an iron man wouldn't be tarnished.

She took the tube out of the box and tossed the box in the sandwich bag. "I should probably wash those scratches before I put this on. Come on into the bathroom with me. We can do both things in there." She stood and put on a good show of nonchalance as she walked past him toward the bathroom.

He didn't buy it. If he had to guess, he'd say she was as keyed up as he was. He followed her through the bedroom and into the bathroom. As they passed the canopy bed, he controlled the urge to reach for her and draw her down onto the mattress. Forget the scratches, forget the massage. He wanted to feel her body against his. He wondered what she'd do.

She turned at the doorway to the bathroom, her gaze straightforward, as if she had no thought whatsoever of getting cozy on that big bed. "Coming?"

"Um, sure." If Kate had been in the movie business she would have intended her question as sexual innuendo and foreplay. But she wasn't from Hollywood. He needed to remember that.

To the right of the doorway stretched a marble counter with two sinks, and on the left was another counter which served as a vanity. The walls behind both counters were mirrored. Hugh's shaving mug and razor lay where he'd left them when she'd rapped on the cottage door. The large oval hot tub beckoned.

Kate set the tube of ointment on the vanity counter and gestured to a velvet cushioned stool positioned in front of it. "This'll be easier if you sit there."

He did as he was told and watched while she ran warm water over a washcloth before lathering it with soap. Then she soaked another washcloth with plain water and laid it on the counter. Her back was to him, but he could see in the mirror, too. As she worked, her breasts shimmied slightly under the tight T-shirt.

Visually tracing the seams of her bra, he located the puckered evidence of hooks and eyes in the middle of her back. As snug as the T-shirt was, he'd be able to unfasten her bra through the shirt without stripping it off. Of course, that might never happen. There were no guarantees here, only possibilities.

When she leaned over, he got a glimpse of her cleavage in the mirror. Cleavage should be no big deal for him anymore. He'd seen the best Tinsel Town had to offer. Yet the gentle rise of Kate's breasts beneath her shirt made his mouth water.

Her shirt rode up in back again, giving him his second view of bare skin above the waistband of her jeans. He was close enough to reach over and touch her there as he'd fantasized while she was checking him in. He gripped his knees, instead. She should set the pace.

She squeezed excess water out of the soapy washcloth and turned to him. "I'll do the one on your forehead first."

"Okay." He sat very still as she combed her fingers through his hair and held it back, exposing the scratch little Dillon had accidentally given him as he flailed in the water. Somebody had forgotten to trim the kid's fingernails.

But Hugh didn't have much time to think about Dillon now. Kate's breasts rose and fell mere inches from his face as she dabbed the soapy cloth over the scratch. The soap smelled like vanilla, but mingled with that was the spicy aroma of her perfume and an undertone of her basic scent.

Sure enough, that last was his favorite. He'd read about pheromones and had dismissed the idea because he'd never experienced that moth-to-the-flame effect the researchers talked about. He was experiencing it now. He wanted to bury his nose between her breasts and take a deep breath.

As she worked he listened to the soft music of her bracelets and the rhythm of her breathing. Her breathing was uneven, and that gave him hope that this encounter would evolve into an outstanding experience before the night was over. He wondered if pheromones worked both ways. What a bummer if he wanted to inhale her scent from top to bottom and she had no such urges.

"Does that hurt?" she murmured.

"No." His nerve endings registered the sting, but he was so busy dealing with his growing arousal that he barely noticed.

"You wouldn't tell me if it did, would you?"

"No."

She sighed, which caused her breasts to tremble invitingly. "That's what I thought. I don't want to hurt you, but I'd hate for these scratches to get infected. You of all people shouldn't let that happen. You'll set a bad example."

He wasn't sure exactly why an infected scratch would set any kind of example to anyone, but he decided not to question her reasoning. Now wasn't the time to disagree with this wonderful creature and risk spoiling the mood. "Don't worry. I heal fast."

"Good." She set the soapy cloth down, picked up the other one and rinsed the soap off his forehead. She wiped carefully, making sure she didn't allow soapy water to drip into his eyes.

He gripped his knees harder. He'd never been this close to a woman he wanted without acting on his impulses.

Then she blew softly on the scratch, her breath sweet and cool, driving him right out of what was left of his mind. He closed his eyes and a sound escaped him—part moan, part whimper.

"I'm hurting you."

"No." What hurt was his penis, which was protesting the confinement of his jeans. He rested his left hand casually in his lap to disguise the evidence.

"Let me put the ointment on. That will take the sting out." She smoothed something creamy over the scratch.

She must have leaned closer because he could feel her heat. He was afraid to open his eyes for fear he'd be looking directly into the scooped neckline of her T-shirt. A guy could only take so much before he cracked.

"That's better," she murmured. "Now for your arm."

From the movement of air, he knew she was no longer hovering quite so close, so he dared to open his eyes.

She held the soapy washcloth in her right hand. "I guess you can stand, now."

No, he couldn't. Not without major groin pain. "How about if I just prop my arm on the counter?" He leaned over and rested his right forearm on the cool marble.

"That works."

Instead of watching her doctor the scratch on his arm, he stared straight ahead and tried to will his erection back down. After the first aid would come the massage, and he'd better not start that procedure already fully aroused.

He tried to remember the last time he'd had such a quick response to a woman and he couldn't think back that far. Maybe it was the environment he worked in. He'd heard that people who worked in a doughnut shop quickly got sick of the doughnuts because they were always available. Beautiful women were always available on a movie set.

Still, it didn't make sense that he'd fly across the country and become instantly attracted to Kate simply because she lived and worked in Providence instead of L.A. He had to go back to the pheromone theory. She smelled...perfect. And he was so turned on he was about to embarrass both of them.

She leaned closer, and he caught his breath.

"There, I knew it. I'm hurting you."

"No, I'm fine."

Her gaze penetrated his. "Then why did you gasp?"

4

HUGH THOUGHT IT WAS TOO soon to tell Kate how much she turned him on. In the movie business he'd learned the value of pacing, and his internal clock told him they needed to spend more time getting to know each other before sex came into it.

That left him with only one explanation for that gasp, and he didn't like it one bit. Still, it was the only option he could think of. "Okay, maybe having you wash out those scratches hurt more than I thought it would." Boy, this was tough, pretending to be a baby.

Her expression warmed. "It's okay to admit to a weakness," she said softly. "We all have them, you know."

"I can't see that you have any." And he sure wished he could.

She shook her head as she recapped the ointment, but she looked pleased, all the same. "Sure I do. I already told you that I run late all the time."

"That doesn't seem so terrible. You'll have to do better than that if you want to convince me you're full of faults."

She leaned her hips against the counter and gazed at him. "I drive too fast. My insurance is through the roof because of my lead foot."

"Mine, too." This didn't seem to be getting them anywhere. The more she revealed, the more he could see that they had matching flaws, so she wouldn't get on his nerves at all.

She put down the ointment and crossed her arms. "I despise working with figures, so I don't balance my checkbook. Kim hates that about me. I keep a general total in my head, and when I get my statement each month I just put in that amount, so I can know approximately where I am. Can you believe anyone would be so undisciplined?"

He could, because he was. "How do you keep from being overdrawn?" He wondered if she used the same method he did.

"I always keep a cushion. Kim says that's wasted money, but I don't care. See? I'm a terrible money manager."

"Terrible," he said, smiling.

"You don't look properly horrified."

"Believe me, I'm horrified." Horrified to discover they were way too much alike. Match that up with the pheromone thing, and he was heading for disaster.

"If you say so." She pushed away from the counter. "Anyway, it's time for your massage. Why don't you get undressed in here?"

Ah, yes. Disaster squared. He should skip the massage, skip the evening he had hoped to enjoy with this tempting woman. True, she lived clear across the continent from him, but the way he was feeling, that wouldn't be far enough. He could go crazy with this one. The danger signs were all there.

"You're hesitating." Her expression grew uncertain. "Have you reconsidered?"

He should definitely reconsider. He might have happened upon the one woman he couldn't protect himself against.

"It's okay." She valiantly tried to keep her disappointment from showing. "I can understand that you wouldn't want to trust your body to an amateur. And we don't have a regular table, so we'd have to use the bed, which isn't as good, I'll admit."

The bed would be outstanding. He couldn't think of anything he'd rather do than be massaged by Kate on a king-size bed.

"Maybe the whirlpool will work out better all the way around." She headed for the bathroom door.

He should just let her go. That would be the best for everyone concerned. He knew that. But pheromones wiped out his reasoning ability. "I'd really rather have you give me a massage," he said. "I hesitated because I'm...shy." *Shy?* Where the hell had that come from? And what a load of bull it was! His friends in L.A. would split a gut laughing if they heard that one.

Kate didn't laugh. Her expression became tender and sweet. "I sensed that about you."

Then her sensors had left the building. Harry, now there was a shy guy. Hugh had fixed him up dozens of times back in high school. But Hugh had been hell on wheels with women from the age of fourteen.

"I hope you don't think I'm too bold, offering to do this," she said.

"No, I think it's a wonderful gesture. I need it desperately." Uh-huh. Like he needed another hole in the head. He might be making the biggest mistake of his life.

She held his gaze. "You might not think so from my attitude, but I have a shy streak, too."

"Really." He could believe that, though. Most of the women he'd known in Hollywood wouldn't have blushed when they proposed to give him a massage.

By Rhode Island standards Kate might be a risk-taker, but not by the yardstick used on the Coast.

"I don't usually let people know that I'm a little shy," she said, "because they might take it for a lack of confidence. In my business you need to project confidence."

"Mine, too," he said.

"Well, your secret's safe with me."

He stared at her, and slowly the truth of it penetrated his sensual haze. He *was* shy—shy about opening up to people and letting his feelings show. His reputation as a bad boy had always preceded him, so no one had ever suspected that he had a tender underbelly of insecurity. But Kate knew nothing about him, and for some reason she'd zeroed right in on the part of his personality he kept hidden, and barely acknowledged himself.

Now that was scary.

"I'll go into the other room and get the massage oil I bought." Her voice was gentle. "Just take off your jeans and your socks and shoes. You can use a towel around your waist if that will make you more comfortable. Then you can stretch out on the bed."

"Okay." A towel would help disguise his condition. "I'd like you to work on my back and shoulders first, if you could." That way he could start the massage on his stomach. What he'd do when she wanted him to turn over was anybody's guess.

"That's fine. I'll be right back."

As she walked out of the bathroom, adrenaline poured through him at the thought of her hands kneading his body. He hadn't been this keyed up since he'd jumped from the Golden Gate Bridge. That time he'd had a net. This time he didn't see one anywhere around.

HE'S THE ONE. Kate trembled as she ripped the shrink-wrap off the basket of massage oils. She had no doubt that she'd finally found her soul mate. She'd told him everything bad about her personality, and he hadn't flinched. In fact, he'd reacted as if he understood all her little quirks perfectly.

On top of that, he was shy. She could imagine as a doctor he had to constantly pretend otherwise or his patients wouldn't trust him to take care of them. But he'd told her the truth, and looking into his eyes she could tell he was a little surprised that he had.

He probably didn't realize yet that they were meant for each other. All he understood, and this was so typical of a man, was that he wanted her. She thought it was so cute the way he tried to hide his sexual interest. Maybe, being shy, he was afraid she wouldn't return his lusty feelings.

She had to let him know that she definitely would. They had so little time alone, and they had to make the most of it. As she pulled the bottle of almond oil from the basket, she thought of the package of condoms in the bottom of her purse. They might be star-crossed lovers, but that didn't mean she should abandon all caution.

Digging through her purse, she glanced over her shoulder to make sure he wasn't standing in the bedroom doorway watching her. He wasn't. No doubt he was already stretched out on the canopy bed, six-feet-plus of pure hero, waiting for her to give him a massage.

She quickly opened the box and took out a condom.

Shoving the box back into her purse, she stood and slid the condom into the front pocket of her jeans. Because her jeans were tight, she could feel the round impression against her hip. She looked to see if it showed and, fortunately, it didn't. Being prepared was one thing. Walking into the bedroom with a distinctive package outlined by her jeans pocket was quite another.

Before starting into the bedroom, she reviewed what she'd learned in her massage class. The excitement of the moment made concentrating on her lessons difficult. Besides, the routine had already been disrupted by her hero insisting that she start with him lying facedown. Usually she began with her subject face up, and she began by massaging fingers and hands, not back and shoulders.

This wouldn't be a textbook massage, then. Nothing wrong with that. No one was here to grade her. Removing her bracelets and her rings, she laid them on the table. Then she drew in a long, shaky breath before walking toward the bedroom. With every step she tried to mentally prepare herself for the sight of him lying on the four-poster.

He would look gorgeous, muscled, and—most irresistible of all—vulnerable. She would have to keep her cool, no matter how tempting he looked, because he really did need the best massage she could manage under the circumstances. So she had to think about massage technique, and remember how to—

Dear sweet heaven, there he was. At her first view of his sculpted body draped casually with a towel, the blood left her head in a rush, coursing through her and settling with a sweet heaviness between her thighs. She'd never had such an instant reaction to a man's semi-naked state, which only confirmed that this was the person she'd waited a lifetime to find.

Her man. Her magnificent man. Her hero. He'd tossed the pillows to the floor and he lay flat on the bed with his eyes closed and his breathing steady. Damn, he might already be asleep. Tactical error on her part. She shouldn't have told him to lie down, because she didn't want him asleep yet. Yes, that was selfish, but how could they bond if he was asleep? Considering what he'd been through, he could easily sleep until morning.

His skin was golden from the sun, something she hadn't noticed until she saw it contrasted against the ivory lace coverlet on the canopy bed. Gazing in fascination at his strong legs, she traced the pattern of the dark hair sprinkled liberally on his calves and more sparsely on his thighs. His toes were long and elegant. Moving closer, she noticed a curved purple scar on his left ankle and another jagged scar on the back of his right knee.

He was obviously a man who took chances, and these scars were the evidence. She'd always wanted a man like that, yet now that she'd found one, the evidence of his daring made her question how well she'd handle the risks he was destined to take. For the first time she wondered if Grandpa Charlie's bravery had seemed reckless and unnecessary to his grieving wife.

One thing was for sure—when a woman got her hands on a bonafide hero, she had to live for the moment. Kate moved closer to the bed while she debated touching him lightly to see if he'd wake up. The edge of the towel had settled between his partially open thighs. She studied the drape of the towel and tried to guess whether or not he'd kept on his underwear. Being shy, he might have done that. She wondered what kind of underwear he might prefer.

"Is anything wrong?"

Her glance flew to his face. His eyes were open. A flush heated her cheeks as she realized he'd been watching her watching him. "I...I thought you were asleep."

"No." His voice was husky and his eyes were that same smoky blue they'd been when she'd roused him from sleep in the car.

All she could think about was sliding onto the bed beside him and snuggling into his arms.

"Am I positioned right?" he asked.

A massage. She was supposed to give him a massage. "You're fine," she said. "Just fine." She slipped out of her mules. "I'll—um—need to climb up there with you in order to get the right leverage."

"I figured."

She looked into his eyes and thought about destiny. If she was right, and all her instincts told her she was, she'd spend a lifetime touching this man. Now was the beginning. She wanted it to be special. "I hope you like the scent of almonds."

He held her gaze. "Love it."

Her stomach bottomed out. "G-good. That's good. That's what I have. Almond oil." So she was babbling like an idiot, which was marginally better than what she really wanted to do—swoop down and kiss him right on those moist, parted lips. His mouth looked so...so capable of giving pleasure.

"Need help getting it open?"

"What?"

"The oil."

"Oh." She glanced at the bottle, the bottle she was

clenching so tightly that her knuckles showed white beneath her skin. "That's okay. I've got it." She twisted off the cap in one motion, releasing the heady scent of almonds into the air. With the adrenaline flooding her system, she could probably unscrew the lug nuts on a tire with her bare hands.

And the way she was quivering, she'd spill the oil all over him as she climbed up on the bed. "Could you hold the bottle for a minute?" It wasn't the smoothest move, to ask the massage subject to hold his own bottle of oil, but at least he wouldn't have to reach far to accomplish it.

"Sure thing." He took the bottle and their hands brushed.

Her stomach dipped again. Whew. If touching by chance brought that reaction, an intentional caress would reduce her to jelly. As often as she'd dreamed of meeting her perfect match, she'd never expected to feel so helplessly attracted that she could barely function. It was embarrassing.

"Ready?" she asked.

He continued to watch her with those warm, smoky eyes. "Whenever you are."

"I'll need to straddle you." And damned if *that* didn't sound far more suggestive than she'd intended.

"Whatever works."

"That's the best way." She'd talked the procedure to death. Now it was time to just do it. Her heart beat so fast that her ears rang, but she worked up her courage and placed one knee on the bed. Then she braced her arms on either side of his waist and swung her other knee over his hips.

There she was, crouched over the most delectable expanse of male muscles she'd ever encountered. She could imagine only two improvements she'd like to make—removing the towel and turning him face up.

"Ready for the oil?"

Right. The oil. She was several miles ahead of herself. She reached for the bottle. "Yes." The brief touch of his hand still affected her, but it was overshadowed by her keen anticipation of smoothing oil over that glorious body. The prospect made her mouth water.

Settling back on her heels, she poured a quarter-sized circle of oil in the palm of her hand, the way she'd been taught. Then she realized she still had a problem with the bottle. She couldn't make him hold it during the massage. Yes, she could ask him to take it back and put it on the nightstand, but he'd have to prop himself up and lean over to do that.

Then she'd have the same problem when she needed more oil. He'd be constantly handing her the bottle. Involving a massage subject in the process to that extent wasn't good form. She was trying to build a mood, and all this bottle business wouldn't help. Time for a little improvisation.

Tilting the bottle, she drizzled oil over his back as if pouring syrup on a stack of pancakes.

He flinched. "That's...chilly."

"Sorry." Damn, she should have warmed it in the microwave. Wiping the oil in her right hand off on his shoulder, she recapped the bottle tightly and laid it on the bed beside her. "I warned you that I'm an amateur."

"No problem. It's warmer, now."

"Good. Let me know if I hurt you." And at last she laid both hands on his back and wondered why she didn't hear a sizzle. He was so warm, so incredibly warm. The scent of almonds mingled with the aroma of healthy male.

He sighed.

That one little sigh set off major tingling and throbbing between her thighs. She became aware of the seam of her jeans pressing against her crotch, and that her legs were conveniently spread apart.

She did her best to ignore her body's response as she smoothed the oil over his skin and leaned forward to knead his neck and shoulders. From that vantage point she could see his face in profile, his dark lashes brushing his bronzed cheekbones, his lips parted. Even the curve of his ear looked erotic to her. She imagined running her tongue over the outer rim and following the spiral around until the tip slid into the downy, shadowed interior.

Her nipples tightened as she caught a whiff of the mint-scented shaving cream he'd used while she was out buying sandwiches and massage oil. *And condoms.* The one in her pocket felt like a brand pressing against the top of her thigh.

She still couldn't believe how solid he was. For a man who worked with a chart and a stethoscope all day he had outstanding muscles. They were knotted and tense, though, and she dug in deeper.

He moaned softly.

"Hurt?" she murmured. She was only too ready to kiss it and make it better.

"Feels...great."

Didn't it, though. Damn, now her panties were wet. She was turning herself on, and yet she was probably putting him into such a relaxed state that he'd drift right off. If that happened, she'd have to go home. Unless she pinched him. Very gently. Just enough to keep him awake.

No, she wouldn't pinch him. Judging from the tightness under his shoulder blades, he needed this massage, and she was glad to give it to him. If he went to sleep, she'd figure out something.

She found another scar on his right shoulder, an older one that had nearly faded into his tan. And there was still another between his ribs, and a third in the small of his back. Apparently rescuing six people from a sinking sailboat was only one of many adventures he'd had.

As she scooted down to pay better attention to his lower back, he shifted his hips slightly, drawing her attention to his towel-draped buns and making her wonder why he'd decided to start this massage on his stomach. *Because he didn't want her to know that he was aroused.*

It was the logical explanation. And it was easily tested.

Heart hammering, she moved still lower and opened the bottle of oil. Slowly she dribbled it on the backs of his thighs. He flinched again as he had when she'd poured oil on his back, but this time he said nothing.

Rising up on her knees, she studied the set of his jaw. Unless she was mistaken, he was clenching it. Her gaze traveled to his hands and discovered he'd closed them both into fists. Apparently she didn't have to worry about putting him to sleep.

She could comment on his tenseness. Or she could capitalize on it. Closing up the bottle, she laid it on the bed and began a slow massage of his right thigh, dangerously close to the hem of the towel. His breathing grew shallow.

As she continued kneading his thigh muscles, she allowed her hands to move close to the towel but never underneath. She could feel his anticipation, wondering if she would honor that barrier. She did. Until she moved to his left thigh.

Once she'd rubbed the oil in well, she started her massage at the top of his thigh. Her chest grew tight as she allowed her fingertips to skim under the hem of the towel. She encountered nothing but bare skin. A flush moved through her and she trembled. There was nothing covering him but a layer of Egyptian cotton toweling.

He groaned.

Her blood pounded through her veins. This was really going to happen between them.

"Kate." His voice was thick with tension.

"Mmm?" It was the best she could do. Her tongue wasn't working at the moment. She waited for him to ask her to make love to him.

"I'm...you need to...stop."

"Stop?" She hadn't expected that word, and it sent her scrambling off the bed in confusion. "What's—what's wrong?"

He opened his eyes, and his gaze smoldered. "Because I'm an idiot."

"I don't under—"

"Your massage has really made me..." A muscle in his jaw worked. "I'm going crazy, Kate. I want you." He ground out the words in obvious frustration.

"That's okay," she said softly. More than okay. Wonderful.

"No, it isn't."

"But it is," she said, "because I—"

"I have no business wanting you."

She swallowed. "Oh?" She wondered what he hadn't told her, what terrible secret he'd been unwilling to reveal that would doom their love before it even started. "Why?"

"Because I'm not prepared, damn it. It just came to me that I am totally not prepared."

She smiled in relief. So that was all. And how herolike that he'd assume the responsibility was all his. Fortunately for him, she had that under control this time. She slipped her hand in her pocket.

"And I'm sure you aren't, either," he said.

She froze in the act of pulling out the condom packet. Maybe he'd think that a woman who brought a condom into a man's bedroom, especially a man she'd just met, was too wild for him. The prudent thing would be to leave and never let on that she'd been so bold.

But she'd never been a fan of the prudent thing. Besides, he might be shy, but he was obviously a daredevil, too. Maybe he'd secretly applaud her courage. And she really, really wanted to be swept away tonight.

"I'm sorry, Kate," he murmured. "I shouldn't have—"

"Look, I want you to know this is unusual for me, and I hope you won't take it the wrong way, but..." She pulled out the condom packet and held it up.

5

HUGH STARED AT THE PACKET in Kate's hand in astonished delight. Wow. This woman was absolutely perfect for him, and he was afraid that, crazy as it seemed, he might be already half in love with her. Fortunately she had all the signs of being an independent woman who took her pleasure where she could find it, someone who didn't expect a commitment before she climbed aboard the fun bus. That sort of liberated attitude should help keep him out of trouble.

"Do you still want me to stop?" she murmured.

Somehow he managed to get the right answer past vocal cords that felt as stiff as his penis. "No. Absolutely not." He rolled to his side and propped himself on one elbow. The towel fell away, but he didn't bother to cover himself. There was no reason to be coy with a lady who carried condoms in her pocket.

Her gaze drifted south, and she caught her breath. "I guess you don't."

He held out his hand and cleared his throat. "I want you to come over here, please."

She took a step toward the bed and hesitated. "So you're not shocked that I came in here with this?" She held up the condom. "You don't think I'm too pushy?"

He shook his head and grinned. "Definitely not too pushy. Maybe a little overdressed, though."

Her green eyes took on a devilish gleam. "Would you like me to fix that?"

"I would love for you to fix that."

"All right." She tossed him the condom, which he caught in midair. "One naked lady, coming up."

He laughed, unable to believe his good fortune. He'd known women who were playful and women who were bold, but he'd never found both qualities in the same lover. He'd have to work very hard not to fall for her. "Kate Cooper, where have you been all my life?"

"Right here." She pulled her T-shirt over her head, tousling her short red curls. "Waiting to see what develops." She tossed the T-shirt away. "That's a photography joke."

"I like it." He liked more than the joke. He'd always thought black lace was the ultimate turn-on, but white lace had just become his favorite, especially when it cupped breasts as plump and inviting as Kate's.

She unsnapped her jeans and pushed them down over her hips. Then she paused and glanced at him. "Should I be doing a Gypsy Rose Lee number for you?"

"Maybe later. Right now I just want all that stuff to disappear. I've been in agony for...a long time."

She did that thing where she stuck her tongue in the corner of her mouth and looked adorable. "I know."

"You *knew*?" He'd worked so hard to keep her from finding out his condition, all for nothing. "When?"

"When I was checking you out in the bathroom and you were looking...lumpy." She stepped out of her jeans.

"Lumpy." Not the most flattering way to describe his package.

"Lumpy is good." She reached behind her back, unfastened her bra and let it slide down her arms.

He moaned in total appreciation. "No, *that* is good." He watched hungrily as she tossed the bra aside. There was no sweeter sight than the gentle sway of a woman's natural breasts. In Hollywood he'd seen far too many that were anything but natural, and he'd never understood the appeal.

As she slipped off her panties, revealing once and for all that she was also a natural redhead, he wondered if he was dreaming. Maybe he'd fallen asleep on the plane and this was his ultimate fantasy playing in his exhausted brain.

She started toward the bed. "Want some help with that?"

He looked at the condom packet that he'd forgotten he held. Then he looked back at her. There was a lot of delicious territory to explore. Maybe he should wait awhile on the main event. He wiggled the dangling packet. "I'm assuming this is the Lone Ranger?"

She met his gaze. "What would you say if I told you there was a whole box in the other room?"

"You're kidding."

"Nope."

"Then I'd have to say you're one hell of a shopper." He assumed she'd bought the darn things while she was out getting sandwiches and was enormously flattened. "And I must have made a *very* good first impression."

"When something's right, it's right."

"I couldn't agree more." Damn, but he loved green eyes. They were the perfect combination of innocence and seduction. "Are you sure this is Rhode Island?"

he murmured, reaching for her hand and pulling her down to the bed.

Her breath caught as she settled beside him and looked up into his eyes. Her voice was low and husky. "Pretty sure."

"I don't think so." He laid the condom aside and cupped her face in his hand. Her skin felt even softer than he'd imagined it would. "I think my plane touched down in heaven." Then he covered her mouth with his.

THEIR FIRST KISS. Kate thought most soul mates probably shared their first kiss before getting naked instead of after, but she wasn't complaining. Naked had some real advantages. Her hero had started by chastely stroking her cheek, but in short order he'd begun stroking the rest of her, and he didn't have to fumble through layers of clothing to get to the good parts.

Neither did she. And the longer they kissed, the more convinced she became that a kiss involving fullbody caressing was the only way that soul mates should begin a relationship. Right away she knew that his hand fit perfectly over her breast and that he understood exactly what to do once he arrived there to bring her to a fever pitch, not that she needed to get any hotter.

But whether she needed the added heat or not, he was giving it to her by the clever way he kneaded her breast and rolled her nipple between his thumb and forefinger. And all the while he was kissing her fullout, and she was doing the same, holding nothing back.

She'd already become intimately acquainted with

his back, so she explored uncharted territory, running her fingers through the springy hairs covering his pecs and massaging his hard little nipples. From there it was a natural progression to move lower and finally touch the source of his agitation for the past hour or more.

Now all that magnificence was causing her a fair bit of agitation, especially when she curled her fingers around it and imagined the kind of pleasure he could give her. She squeezed gently, and he moaned low in his throat. When she brushed her thumb under the small ridge at the very tip, he drew his mouth from hers for the first time.

He gulped for air. "Careful," he warned.

She nibbled at his lower lip as she caressed him again. She was getting impatient for that ultimate bonding, where their fate would be sealed forever, when they would know without any doubt that this was the person they'd been born to love. "I don't want to be careful. I want to be wild."

"Is that right?" He slipped his hand between her thighs. When he found her drenched and ready, he sucked in a breath.

"Put on the condom," she whispered, nipping at his mouth.

With a groan he pulled away from her and found the packet. Then she watched him tear it open and roll the condom over his straining penis. She doubted he understood the significance of what they were about to do, but once they were locked together, he might get a glimmer of the truth.

He moved over her, his gaze hot. "You're incredible."

"We're incredible." She concentrated on his stormy blue eyes. "Make love to me."

"My pleasure." His tone was light as he sank into her. But once they were locked together, the playfulness disappeared from his expression. "Oh, Kate. Kate, this is..."

"I know. Perfect."

"Yeah." Wonder filled his eyes.

"I knew it would be." She welcomed every last inch as her body opened to him. Undulating waves of pleasure signaled that her orgasm hovered near, and she gripped his bottom to hold him deep inside her as she tilted her face up to his.

He started to close his eyes.

"Don't," she whispered. "Don't close your eyes."

His dark lashes fluttered, and then he looked at her with a mixture of awe and fear. "You're blowing me away. You know that, don't you?"

"Yes."

"I never thought...."

"Don't think." She lifted her hips and urged him closer. "Just feel."

His eyes darkened. "Hold still."

"I can't."

"I'll come."

She held his gaze. "And so will I."

With a groan he drew back and plunged deep once more. "So good." He gasped and stroked again. Then he hesitated, his whole body quivering. "Kate, I don't want this to end. Let me—"

"Don't stop."

With a strangled cry he pushed home, propelling them both to a tumultuous climax.

HUGH LAY WITH HIS HEAD on Kate's shoulder and struggled for breath while he tried to convince himself that his whole world hadn't just tilted on its axis. Right now he might think that was the most amazing orgasm of his life, but he was exhausted and jet-lagged. Kate was wonderful—no doubt about that—but she wasn't necessarily the most terrific woman he would ever meet.

His weekend promised to be an experience to remember, but come Sunday he'd fly out of Providence without a twinge of remorse. At the moment he couldn't imagine saying goodbye to her, but once he'd had some sleep that neediness would disappear. Sleep deprivation messed with a person's head. He'd read that somewhere.

Kate stroked his back. "You need to rest, now."

He nodded, his cheek rubbing against her shoulder. Reluctantly he eased away from her, climbed from the bed and stumbled into the bathroom. When he returned she'd folded the sheets back and she stood, still naked, beside the canopied bed. He'd carry that mental picture around with him for a while.

Memories were good. He had a head full of great memories, and this weekend would certainly spice up the old mental scrapbook. Gratitude rushed through him in a warm flood. Or maybe it was more than gratitude. His penis twitched.

He gave voice to the first emotion. "Thank you," he said. "That was—"

"I know." She stepped forward and placed a finger on his lips. "You don't have to say a word. Words don't really do justice to what happened, anyway."

"You're right." He gazed at her rosy breasts and his penis twitched again.

"You need sleep," she said.

He'd thought so a few minutes ago. Now he wasn't so sure that's how he'd choose to spend his time.

"I think I should go home and let you sleep for the rest of the night."

"No, don't." His answer was too quick and sounded too desperate. He'd need to work on that between now and Sunday. "We'll have so little time together once we get into the wedding activities," he added.

She wound her arms around his neck, and sleep moved way down on his priority list. "I thought that, too, but I'm worried about you getting enough rest."

He drew her into his arms and felt that dangerous longing again, that sense of rightness and forever that he'd taken great pains to avoid. Maybe keeping her here all night wasn't a smart thing. "Let me worry about that," he said, proving that his brain had no clout whatsoever.

Slipping away from him, she glanced at his gradually thickening penis and smiled. "I won't leave, but maybe I'll step out of the room for a little while so you can climb into bed and try to sleep."

"If you're going to step out of the room, you can go find that box you mentioned."

"All right." She tried to look stern and commanding. "But you'd better be in that bed by the time I come back."

"I can't think of anywhere I'd rather be." And that in itself was scary. Hugh thought about that as he slid between the soft ivory sheets, because he'd been to a lot of cool places in his career. The movies he'd made had taken him in canoes down the Amazon and into the cracked heart of a glacier in Alaska. He'd scouted for rhinos on the Serengeti and ridden horseback across the Mongolian Steppes. For fifteen years his life had been a series of thrills.

And yet…sinking deep inside Kate a few minutes ago had them all beat. No doubt that was his giddy exhaustion talking, though. If he could try it again, he'd probably discover having sex with her wasn't such a big deal.

He glanced toward the sitting room, impatient for her to come back to bed. "What are you doing in there?"

"Straightening up," she said. "Relax for a few minutes. I'll be right there."

He lay staring up at the dark wood slats supporting the white brocade canopy while he fought to stay awake. She would be back any second, and she was bringing condoms. He didn't want to go to sleep at a time like this. Maybe later, after he'd made love to her again, he'd catch a few zees. But first he wanted to give himself a reality check so that he could stop worrying.

When he opened his eyes, the room was dark. Damn, he had fallen asleep, after all. A faint glow seeped around the edge of the curtains at the window, and he figured the security lights outside were causing it, because it definitely wasn't morning. He'd be hearing birds if that was sunlight on the other side of those curtains.

Cautiously he turned his head on the pillow, not wanting to find that she'd decided to leave, after all, once she found him dead to the world. Apparently she was a woman of her word, because there she was, the sheet pulled over her shoulder and her cheek nestled into the pillow beside him.

He was glad to have her there. Then the reality of that sank in. *He was glad to have her there.* Usually he felt hemmed in when he ended up sleeping in the same bed with a woman. Sex was one thing, but sharing the covers through the night hours was a whole new ball game for him.

For one thing, he didn't like to advertise that he had nightmares. They could come at any time, but the most likely was near the anniversary of his brother Joe's death. Fortunately that was months away, yet. After eighteen years they should have disappeared, and they were fewer now, but they still happened.

The dream was always the same. He walked down a street and came upon the twisted wreck that had been Joe's car. Joe was inside, and Hugh couldn't get him out, even though he knew Joe was dying. He woke up yelling and trying to claw the covers to bits.

A couple of times he'd been unlucky enough to have the nightmare when someone was sharing his bed, and he'd always passed it off as the kind of bad dream brought on by all the risks he took as a stuntman. But he didn't like lying, so he'd worked to avoid the problem by not falling asleep until he was alone in his bed.

Tonight the rewards had seemed well worth the risk, but he still couldn't get over the rush of pleasure he'd felt when he'd discovered Kate lying next to him. Propping his head on his fist, he gazed at her in the dim light. He studied the mouth that had given him such a jolt when he'd started kissing her.

Kissing hadn't been that much fun in years, and yet there was nothing unusual about her mouth. Her lower lip was pouty and full, while her upper lip had that sweet little dent in the middle. It was just a mouth, like the dozens he'd kissed over the years. Nothing about the shape of her mouth explained why he was lying here with saliva pooling on his tongue and wishing he could kiss her right now, right this very minute.

But he should let her sleep. She was the maid of honor, and beginning tomorrow she'd have all kinds of duties to perform for Kim. At least he supposed she would. He was no expert in this wedding business. Selfishly he hoped there wouldn't be a whole lot for her to do, because then he could lure her back to this cozy little cottage and work on emptying that box she'd mentioned.

He wondered if she'd brought it into the bedroom, or if she'd deliberately stayed out in the sitting room until he'd dozed off and left the box in there. She'd been pretty set on him getting some sleep. He squinted at the nightstand on her side of the bed. Yeah, that could be a condom box lying there. In this light he couldn't tell for sure.

"You're awake." Her voice sounded drowsy, but friendly. More than friendly.

He looked down and saw the sparkle of her eyes as she lay there watching him. "You stayed away until I fell asleep."

"Uh-huh. You needed it."

He settled down next to her and slipped his arm under the covers to draw her close. Damn, but she fit nicely against him. "That's not all I need."

She chuckled. "So I just found out."

"Did you bring the box in here?"

"It's on the bedside table." She started to turn over. "I can—"

"Wait." He gripped her tighter. "We're going to do

things a little differently this time. That first session was way too short." And way too powerful. Maybe if he slowed the pace he'd diffuse some of the emotion that had hit him the moment he'd joined his body with hers.

"I had no complaints." She nuzzled his neck.

"Neither did I." He rolled her to her back. "But variety is the spice of life." That had been a guiding principle of his for years.

"You don't like to be bored, do you?"

"No." He nipped gently at her earlobe. "And neither do you. That's why you're moving away from studio photography to the challenge of candid shots." He'd told himself not to talk about that, not to get involved. He couldn't seem to help it.

She rubbed her hands over his back in a light massage. "I'm not moving away from studio photography."

"Are too." He brushed his body lazily back and forth across hers and breathed in the scent of her arousal.

"It's a side interest. A hobby." She traced a path under his right shoulder blade. "Where did you get the scar you have here?"

"Fell out of a moving Jeep and landed on a railroad tie." He kissed the swell of her breast.

"Doing what?"

"It was a robbery."

"A *robbery?*" She stiffened beneath him. "What do you mean?"

He was hovered over the dark promise of her nipple. There were so many treats that he'd bypassed earlier. "Could we talk about it later?"

"But—"

"Please." Then he leaned down and closed his mouth over her nipple. She didn't ask about the robbery after that. She was much too busy moaning.

Determined to set a leisurely pace, he made sure he paid a generous amount of attention to each full breast before moving lower. Once he'd nestled his head between her silken thighs, he took his own sweet time there, too. Judging from her reaction, he figured it was time well spent.

From his vantage point, he'd loved every tasty minute, and he might have lingered a while longer if she hadn't started begging for the thrust of his penis. He couldn't deny her, and he was close to bursting, anyway, so it was probably a good idea.

Once he'd fumbled his way through the condom application, he discovered that burying his penis inside her was a *very* good idea, possibly the idea of the millennium. But if he'd hoped that the moment would lack the punch of that first time, those hopes were dashed. If anything, the feeling of sliding into her hot body was more spectacular than ever.

At least this time, with the help of a little sleep, he had some stamina, but his climax teased him mercilessly as he stroked back and forth, hoping to make her come again. And he would, he realized quickly. He'd never been so in tune with a woman in his life. Either he'd suddenly become the most accomplished lover in the world, or he and Kate had something very special going.

As he led her to the brink and effortlessly managed to time his orgasm to hers, he knew the answer to that question. It wasn't the answer he wanted.

6

AT DAWN KATE WOKE WITH thoughts of the huge whirlpool tub on her mind. She and her hero had made spectacular, full-throttle love three times during the night, and although he continued to sleep soundly, she was wide awake and ready for a refreshing soak. But she didn't want to disturb her sleeping prince.

As it was she didn't think he'd had nearly enough rest. She'd coaxed him back to sleep after their second go-round, but after another catnap, he'd roused her with kisses for a third romp. Resisting him had been out of the question, especially when he'd slid his fingers deep inside her and discovered how ready she was.

Thinking about that made her hot all over again. Lying beside him and fighting the urge to reach for him didn't sound like a fun way to spend the next couple of hours. She shifted her weight and watched his face for signs that he was waking up. His smooth, shallow breathing never changed.

Damn, but he was a handsome guy. His dark hair lay in soft waves over his forehead and she longed to comb it back with her fingers and kiss him awake. She'd love to watch as desire grew hot in his blue eyes. They'd never made love in daylight.

But he really needed his sleep. Keeping her gaze on him, she slid carefully out from under the covers and eased off the edge of the bed. Her toes touched the fine Oriental carpet beside the bed. So far, so good. As she tiptoed carefully around the bed toward the bathroom, her lover slept on.

Once inside the spacious bathroom, she quietly closed the double doors to shut out the sound of water running into the tub. From the moment she'd first seen this bathroom on the inspection tour with Kim, she'd lusted for this whirlpool. With a touch of a button she raised the translucent blinds covering the windows looking out on the private rose garden. Sunlight streamed into the room and glanced off the ivory tub and gold faucets.

Kate wasn't hung up on luxuries in general, but she had a weakness for sports cars and extravagant bathtubs. So far she'd only been able to indulge one of her weaknesses with the Miata, but apartment living meant she'd had to postpone enjoyment of her second. This morning she could temporarily remedy that lack.

Closing the drain, she turned on the water and adjusted the temperature so it was slightly hotter than she'd need it to be eventually. She glanced at the jets, anticipating with relish the pleasure of that liquid massage. With six of those little honeys she'd forgo the bubble bath. Once she'd made the mistake of adding a generous amount of bubbles to a tub before turning on the jets, and she'd foamed the entire bathroom by the time she reached the off switch.

While the tub filled, she ran through some basic stretching exercises. What fun to make love to a man who was as limber as she was. Their last time together had turned into a fairly athletic enterprise. They'd both ended up laughing as they challenged each other to maintain some tricky positions.

Then the laughter had faded away as they'd returned to that magic rhythm that was theirs alone. She shouldn't be surprised that they were so sexually compatible. Soul mates should be. Yet it still inspired wonder each time they rediscovered how perfect they were for each other.

At last the water level suited her. Flipping on the timer for the jets, she went up the tiled step and eased into the hot water, allowing her skin to adjust to the temperature gradually. The tub had two seats, and she settled slowly onto one of them, positioning her lower back against a pulsing jet. Then she grabbed a towel from the stack that had been placed on the ledge surrounding the tub, rolled it up and placed it behind her neck.

Ah. This was the life. Kim thought it was a real contradiction that Kate relished lounging in a whirlpool when normally she lived her life at breakneck speed. Kate had tried to explain that a manic pace dovetailed perfectly with whirlpool jets and massage. Yin and yang. Kim said if Kate would slow down a little, she wouldn't need to unwind. Kate knew she'd go crazy in a constant state of unwind.

As she closed her eyes and let her thoughts flow with the swirling water, she considered how best to let her family know of this sudden bond she'd created with the best man. There was no point in trying to keep it a secret, at least not from Kim. Twins couldn't get away with that.

So she'd tell Kim first, who could inform Stuart. Maybe they could contain the information right there for a while. Once Kate's mom knew, she'd start planning the next wedding, and Kate wasn't ready for that. Besides, Harry hadn't even proposed.

But he would. Kate couldn't imagine any other possibility. After all, he'd asked her where she'd been all his life. That was a very telling thing to say. He might even ask her to marry him when he woke up this morning, before they went out to face the rest of the wedding guests. After the way they'd made love last night, she wouldn't be surprised.

The bathroom doorknob turned with a soft click, and she opened her eyes. Her hero was awake. Her pulse rate picked up immediately.

"Kate?" he called through the partially open door. "Are you indecent?"

"Absolutely. I'm in the tub. Care to join me?"

"Sounds like a plan." He walked into the bathroom.

"Hey, you," she murmured. What a specimen he was. "That's a good look, by the way."

He smiled, and if he'd been shy before, he'd lost all shyness now. "I'm partial to your outfit, too." He stepped into the tub. "Mmm. Perfect temperature."

"There's another seat over there."

"Too far away." He knelt in the swirling water right in front of her and braced his arms on the edge of the tub, caging her with his body. "I can't kiss you from over there."

"Good point." She leaned forward and wrapped her damp arms around his neck. "Caution. I'm slippery when wet."

"I already know that." He drew closer. "Good morning."

"Isn't it, though?"

"Outstanding morning." Then he kissed her and improved what was already turning out to be a great day.

In no time they were breathing hard and kissing

with such desperation anyone would think they hadn't enjoyed sex with each other in weeks. He scooped Kate up and traded positions, so that he was on the seat and she was balanced on his knees.

Reluctantly she broke away from his kiss. "We can't..."

"I know. Later." Holding her by her waist, he shifted on the seat. "Tell me when you can feel the jet."

"Which jet?" she murmured. "I don't—" Then he moved again, and she knew exactly which jet. She gasped with pleasure.

He smiled with satisfaction. "That jet."

"Oh, my."

"Don't let me block it." He slid two fingers into her, smooth as silk. "You are *very* slippery when wet."

"Mmm." She couldn't talk with all that pleasure going on.

"Still feel the jet?"

She nodded.

"Now touch me, Kate."

Then she understood his plan. Gripping his shoulder with her right hand, she reached beneath the water and wrapped her hand around his ramrod straight penis.

He groaned and closed his eyes. "Yeah. Like that."

"And this?" She slid her hand upward.

He opened his eyes and focused his hot gaze on her. "Uh-huh. While I do this." He eased his fingers back and forth.

"We can...watch each other come."

"Together."

"Yes." Her heart raced.

"Let's...let's make it last."

She nodded, not sure how long she'd be able to hold out between the pulsing of the jet and his rhythmic caress. Sliding her hand up and down his penis and watching the tension build in his expression made her hotter yet.

"Stop," he murmured, closing his eyes again.

"You, too." She was nearly there.

He swallowed and opened his eyes. His jaw muscles flexed, and his voice was thick with desire. "Now go slow."

"You'd better...too." Balanced on the brink of an orgasm and knowing he was right there with her brought an intensity of sensation she'd never known before.

"Easy."

"Mmm." She felt her control slip a notch.

"So sweet. So very—" He moaned. "Kate, I can't—"

"I know. I'm—"

"Yes. Now. Now!" He stroked her quickly, pushing deep.

She increased the pressure of her grip, caressing him faster, and faster yet. When the explosion came, she cried out in astonished pleasure as the delayed climax rocketed through her with unbelievable force. His moan of surrender followed, and she watched in dazed wonder as he gave in to the power of his orgasm and gasped for air, shuddering beneath her hand.

At last they collapsed against each other and let the swirling water soothe the fever they'd created. The pulsing jets rocked them gently, bringing them slowly back to reality. The timer clicked off, and the water grew still. Only the sound of their breathing filled the warm moist air.

Kate didn't hear her cell phone right away, but eventually the familiar little tune penetrated her fog of sensual overload.

"Cell phone," he muttered against her shoulder.

"Mine." She extricated herself from the tangle they'd made of arms and legs intertwined.

"You won't make it."

"I know." She climbed out of the tub on rubbery legs. "But whoever it is will put a message on my pager. I need to find out who that was, in case something important has come up about the wedding."

"I guess so."

"You know I'd rather stay tucked away in this room all day." She pulled an ivory bath sheet from a rack near the tub and wrapped herself in it.

"But we can't."

"Nope." She sighed and started out of the room. Then she remembered that they hadn't discussed what to say once they both left the cottage. She turned back to him. "Um, do you think we should let anyone know we...well, that we've..." She paused, not sure what sort of label to put on what they'd shared.

"Had a fantastic time together?" He gazed at her. "I'll leave that up to you. For my part, I don't care who knows about it. But you know the rules of the game here in Rhode Island better than I do."

She smiled, appreciating his gentlemanly concern. "We'll see how it goes. But I've never been able to keep anything major from Kim."

"However you want to deal with it is fine with me."

"Thanks." She loved the way he was deferring to her on this, but that kind of sensitivity was part of what made her so sure they were meant for each other. "Oh, and when I come back, I want to hear about that robbery you foiled."

"I didn't really—"

"I'll be the judge of that." She could tell he was ready to make light of his contribution, but she wouldn't let him get away with it. "I want to know why you fell out of a moving Jeep. See, I don't forget these things, much as you try to minimize them."

"It really wasn't—"

"Later. And don't think I'll forget." What a hero, she thought as she padded barefoot out to the sitting room and dug around in her purse for her pager. Sure enough, Kim's number showed up on the display.

Kate glanced at the digital clock on the microwave in the kitchen area. No wonder it was Kim. It was already nine-thirty in the morning, and Kim had said she and Stuart would take an early ferry back from Block Island. They had several details to take care of on this last day before the wedding.

Kate wanted to help with her share of those details. She really did. Getting married was huge in a person's life, and Kate wanted the wedding to be absolutely perfect. But she hoped that lightning wouldn't strike her for wishing that she could somehow spend the day getting to know her hero better.

That wouldn't be possible, especially because Harry needed to get together with Stuart for whatever errands had to be accomplished in that quarter. Tuxes needed to be picked up, for one thing, and then there was Stuart's dad's new wife, who was a strict vegetarian. Somebody had to find out if the restaurant they'd chosen for the rehearsal dinner served anything besides seafood.

Kate located her cell phone and dialed Kim's number, but she had trouble keeping her mind on the subject of the wedding. The endless wedding concerns all seemed so unimportant compared to this amazing connection she and Harry had just made. It was time for her to find a pet name for him, too, because she had so much trouble thinking of him as Harry. He didn't act anything like a man named Harry would act.

Kim answered right away.

"Hi," Kate said. "What's up?" She tried to sound like her old self, but she knew Kim would hear something in her voice unless her sister was too stressed about the wedding to have her sensors working.

"You're upset with me, aren't you?" Kim said. "But I swear I didn't know a thing about it until Stuart and I got back from Block Island."

Kate was confused. "Uh, what are you talking about?"

"Harry! Here we begged you to pick him up and keep him entertained for us, and God knows how long you waited at the airport, because he put the message on Stuart's pager, which Stuart left at home because he didn't want interruptions while we were making our great escape, so—"

"Kim, I didn't have to wait at the airport. I don't know what you're talking about."

"So you found out that Harry isn't flying in until today? How did you do that?"

Kate pinched herself to make sure this wasn't some crazy prewedding dream. The pinch hurt, so she had to assume she was awake. Maybe her sister had totally lost track of who was doing what. That could happen.

"Kim," she said patiently. "Harry flew in yesterday. He's here. I picked him up in Warwick yesterday afternoon."

"That's not possible."

"Okay, sweetie, I know you're under a strain and you might be a wee bit confused, but just accept the fact that Harry's in Newport. Stuart's best man is good to go." *In more ways than one.*

"Kate, he can't be. Harry called Stuart from the plane ten minutes ago. He had trouble rescheduling his flight, but he's on his way from O'Hare right now. We're heading out to get him in a few minutes."

Kate's stomach began to churn. "Then...then who did I pick up yesterday afternoon?" Surely she hadn't just spent a wild and crazy night getting jiggy with a complete stranger. "I swear he looked exactly like the picture you gave me! And he knew all about the wedding, and—"

"Omigod, I know who it is!"

"Who?" Kate screeched into the phone as she clutched the towel around her and thought of all the things she'd done with a man she didn't even know. A man who was even now naked in the whirlpool.

"It's Harry's twin brother! Stuart said he might be coming in from L.A."

Twin brother? L.A.? She'd never been to L.A., and somehow that seemed to make this nightmare even worse. "You never told me Harry had a twin!"

"Sure I did."

"Swear to God, Kim, you did not tell me! I would have remembered something like that. Good Lord. I can't believe this."

Kim started laughing. "I'm sorry, Kate. I can't believe I didn't mention it, either, except things have been so frantic, and nobody really thought the guy would show up, so I must have figured it wasn't important."

"Maybe not to *you*, but—" Kate caught herself before she said anything incriminating. She'd probably already way overreacted for someone trying to keep her misdeeds to herself.

"I know. It's embarrassing, and I am sorry. You must have confused the heck out of him if you kept calling him Harry."

But she hadn't, because she hadn't liked the name. She started to shake.

"So you dropped him at the Townsend House, right?" Kim asked.

"Um, yeah."

"See, that's fine. If he got Harry's room by mistake we can always adjust the situation when we get there. No problem. Don't worry about it. This'll make a great story."

"No, it won't!" Kate didn't care if she sounded frantic. She had to stop Kim from spreading the news. "Promise me you won't tell anyone else about this. Cross your heart and hope to die."

"Kate?" Kim stopped laughing. "Kate, what's wrong?"

"Nothing. Nothing's wrong."

"Yes, it is. I can hear it in your voice. Listen, don't feel bad about this. It's not your fault, and I'll make sure nobody teases you. It's an innocent mistake."

No, it's not. There's not a single innocent thing about this mistake. "I'd just rather you didn't make a big deal of it."

"This isn't like you. You like a good joke more than anybody I know. What's the matter, Katy? Is this wedding thing freaking you out?"

"No! I'm fine with the wedding. I love that you're marrying Stuart."

"Are you sure? Because I want you to know that we'll be as close as we ever were. Marriage doesn't have to come between two sisters, as long as they—"

"Kim, that's not the problem!" She couldn't have Kim believing that she had reservations about this wedding that would make her sister so happy. "Trust me, I'm thrilled that you've found Stuart." Her eyes burned. And she thought she'd found her hero, too. "I just didn't get a good night's sleep last night."

"Hmm." Kim wasn't buying it. "I think something's going on. It's about Hugh, isn't it? Something's happened."

"Hugh?"

At that very moment her hero appeared in the sitting room doorway, a towel draped around his hips.

He gave her a questioning glance. "What?"

Kate stared at him. His name was Hugh. But knowing his name didn't change the fact that she'd abandoned herself to a man she knew nothing about. Yet one thing hadn't changed. Unless he'd lied to her, he was a hero who had saved six people in a boating accident.

"Hugh is Harry's twin," Kim said. "You must not have talked to him very much or you would have found out he wasn't Harry. I mean, Harry's an obstetrician and Hugh's a stuntman out in Hollywood. That's why Harry didn't think Hugh would make it to the wedding, because the filming for his latest movie is way behind schedule."

"A stuntman," Kate said tonelessly. Not a hero.

"Uh-huh. That's kind of cool, don't you think? He's in a disaster-at-sea movie starring Antonio Banderas. Hugh got the job as his double because he looks so much like him, except for the eyes. For the stunts they don't photograph him close enough to see the eyes, anyway."

"Guess not." Kate gazed at the man who was not Harry and not a hero. He was Hugh, a stuntman from Hollywood. And she had just made a colossal fool of herself.

"Okay, I get what this is about," Kim said. "You picked up the man you thought was Harry, and it turns out you don't like him. You guys got into a fight about politics, right? I know how you can get if somebody pushes your buttons."

Kate had the inappropriate urge to start laughing, but she was afraid once she started, she'd soon progress into hysterics. "No." She heard her voice quiver. "We didn't get into a fight." *We might now, but we certainly didn't before, when I thought he was Harry.*

Kim sighed. "Then I don't know why you're acting weird. I—oh, can you hold on a minute? Stuart wants to ask me something."

"Sure."

Hugh started to walk toward her, his gaze warm. She held up her hand like a traffic cop. He paused and frowned.

"I'm back," Kim said. "And I have a favor to ask. You can turn me down if you want."

"What?"

"Well, after we pick up Harry at the airport, Stuart needs to take him straight to the tux shop and get that taken care of. And there are some other little details those two have to work out, so it'll be a while before they arrive in Newport. Close to the time of the rehearsal, actually."

"And?"

"And Hugh will be hanging around with nothing to

do. He doesn't know anybody, and because he made the effort to fly all the way here, Stuart doesn't want him to feel unwelcome."

A snort of laughter escaped from Kate. She couldn't help it. If Hugh felt unwelcome it wasn't her fault. She'd *so* welcomed him.

"Kate? What's going on, girl?"

"I choked on some coffee."

"Because you were drinking it too fast, I'll bet. Anyway, Stuart was wondering if you'd be willing to entertain Hugh for the rest of the day, but if you guys really didn't hit it off, feel free to say no."

Kate couldn't believe it. This fiasco kept getting worse and worse. "Don't you need me to help you? There were about half-a-dozen things that we—"

"Mom was driving me crazy because she needed something to do, so I assigned most of those jobs to her. What she doesn't get accomplished, Stuart's mom is going to handle."

"Are you sure that's going to work? I mean, you know how Mom can get."

"I can handle her. Maureen wants to do something, too, and Stuart's sisters. The point is, there are a ton of people around to run errands, Kate, but I wouldn't feel right asking any of them to keep Hugh company for the day. Now that you've met him, you seem like the logical one, and it would really put Stuart's mind at ease. But if you don't want to, I'll under—"

"I'll take care of it." As her panic receded, she was able to realize that the longer she kept Hugh away from the other wedding guests, the less time there would be for people to find out what had gone on between them. If she drove back to Providence today and left him here, no telling what sort of compromising conversation he'd get himself into.

Fortunately she didn't *have* to go back to her place. Her maid of honor dress was already hanging in one of the Townsend House storeroom closets, along with the bridesmaids' dresses and Kim's vintage gown. She had a suitcase full of casual clothes in the closet. She was free to stay in Newport, spend the day with Hugh, and rehearse treating him like a stranger. Which he was.

And she had done all sorts of unthinkable things with this stranger. She had to swear him to secrecy, and if they spent the day together, they could make sure they both had the same story.

"Thanks, Kate," Kim said. "You're the best. Sorry about the mix-up."

"These things happen." But Kate had never, ever had anything happen even remotely like this. "See you this afternoon for the rehearsal."

"Right. Um, Kate?"

"What?"

"We won't be able to start the rehearsal till you get there, so—"

"I won't be late." And she wouldn't be, either, because too many people would be inconvenienced. At the moment she sort of wanted to inconvenience Kim, who had neglected to tell her something that had turned out to be extremely crucial. But she wouldn't hold up the entire wedding rehearsal to get revenge.

"Thanks," Kim said.

"You're welcome."

"See, you're still ticked. I should've remembered to mention Hugh. I just didn't think it would be—"

"It's okay." Kate wanted to lay the blame on her sister, but she knew that wasn't fair. Kim couldn't have known how the mix-up would turn out. "Really, it's fine."

"I hope so."

"It is. Now go pick up Harry." Kate said goodbye and disconnected the phone.

"Who was that?" the stranger named Hugh asked.

"My sister." She looked at him and tried to work up some righteous indignation against him, but none of this was his fault, either. He'd never lied to her. She'd made assumptions and based a whole fiction on those wrong assumptions.

Worse than that, he didn't know that she'd acted on erroneous information. He must think she was quite a swinging chick, offering massages and condoms right off the bat. She had no idea what to say to him. She'd never been more thoroughly embarrassed in her life.

7

HUGH UNDERSTOOD THAT something dramatic had changed in his relationship with Kate, and it had to do with the news she'd received from her sister. "Is the wedding still on?" he asked, thinking that if Kim and Stuart had broken up at the last minute that would throw anybody into a funk.

"It's still on." Holding her towel securely around her with one hand, she tucked her phone into her purse with the other. Then she turned back to him, the strangest expression on her face. "No problems with the wedding, at least."

"What do you mean, *at least?*" He felt like a biology specimen under a microscope. "What's wrong? I can tell that something's totally whacked about this operation."

She continued to look shell-shocked. "Listen, um, *Hugh,* we need to talk, but I'd feel a whole lot better about doing that if we both had our clothes on."

Uh-oh. The party was over, but damned if he knew why. He also wondered why she'd said his name like that, as if she had a hard time getting it out. Now that he thought about it, she hadn't said his name all that much. Make that never, except just now, on the phone.

"So I'm getting dressed," she said.

"I don't understand. What did Kim have to say that would completely change your attitude toward me?"

"It's...it's complicated." She held the towel protectively around her, as if she didn't want to show him an inch more of her body than was absolutely necessary.

This from a woman who had stripped for him without hesitation, who'd invited him into her bathtub and had allowed him to do all sorts of delicious things with her naked, wet body. The more he thought about that, the hotter he became. Yet she seemed to have lost all desire for him.

"Okay." He couldn't fight what he didn't understand, and apparently once they were dressed, he'd get his explanation. "I take it you want to dress somewhere private?"

"If you don't mind. I'd like to have the bathroom."

He wanted to say, *You mean the same bathroom where you so recently came unglued?* But he didn't think she'd react well to that, so he decided to play along for now. "All right." He glanced at the tiny kitchen adjacent to the sitting room. "How about if I make us some coffee?"

She nodded. "Good idea. But putting on your clothes is more important than coffee."

"Oh, I promise to do that, too. I wouldn't want to offend your sensibilities." Yes, he sounded a little sarcastic, but he thought he was allowed. He'd been jerked right out of paradise and he had no idea what he'd done to deserve it.

"Thanks." With one last glance at him, she picked up her oversize purse and walked quickly out of the room. He heard the closet doors open, and he figured she was getting out her suitcase. Then the double bathroom doors closed with a soft click.

He might be mistaken, but he could swear there was another click, as if she'd locked the doors, too. Son of a bitch. Shaking his head, he went into the tiny kitchen area and started filling the coffee carafe with water. How could she have gone from complete trust to wary suspicion in the space of only a few minutes?

Too bad he didn't know the players better. Maybe Kim hadn't been a part of Harry and Stuart's plan to set him up with Kate. He thought about that as he poured the water into the coffeemaker and dropped the packet of premeasured grounds in the basket. Maybe Kim disapproved of her sister hanging out with a love 'em and leave 'em guy like him, and she'd convinced Kate to cut and run.

But he still couldn't believe that Harry and Stuart would have sent Kate to the airport without warning her that he was something of a playboy. Stuart, especially, wouldn't be taking that kind of chance with his bride's twin sister.

Nothing made sense. With a sigh he walked into the bedroom. "I'm getting dressed in here," he called out. "Better wait for the all clear before you open the door or you're liable to catch me without any pants on." How stupid. Thirty minutes ago they'd been giving each other an incredible orgasm, and now she was acting like a damned virgin.

He hoped she didn't have some sort of mental problem. He'd hate to think she was cursed with some sort of multiple personality thing, but it was always possible. Yet he couldn't imagine anyone sending her to the airport to pick him up if they thought she might go schitzy on him. And Stuart and Kim had definitely sent her to the airport. He distinctly remembered her saying they had.

While pulling on his jeans, he noticed the condom box sitting on the bedside table next to where she'd slept. She'd bought those things, damn it! He might have a reputation for being a little wild with the ladies, but he wasn't the one who'd come into this setup armed with condoms.

The more he thought about her revised attitude, the angrier he became. All he'd done was go along with the program. She had no reason to be miffed at *him*, for God's sake. He was the one who should be ticked off at *her*. Which he was, except that he still wanted her with an embarrassing desperation.

After buttoning his jeans, he took a clean T-shirt from the small pile he'd tucked in the top drawer of the dresser and pulled it over his head. "I'm decent, now," he called out. "And the coffee should be about ready. I'll meet you in the sitting room."

Barefoot, he walked back into the kitchen area. Too bad things had turned sour. This place was gorgeous, with the hardwood floors and thick Oriental carpets. He'd had visions of making love to her on one of the carpets. And on the brocade love seat. And up against the table. Anywhere and everywhere.

Unfortunately, those prospects were looking extremely dim. He found a couple of coffee mugs in a cupboard and, wonder of wonders, some of those little restaurant thimbles of real cream in the miniature refrigerator. A bowl of fruit sat on the counter, but he figured the fruit was fake. Picking up a pear that he thought was wax, he discovered it was real and decided to eat it.

"I'm back."

He turned, chewing his bite of pear. She stood beside the table where they'd eaten their dinner, a doomed expression clouding her lovely green eyes. He swallowed the mouthful of pear, tore off a sheet of paper towel and put the pear down on it. "How do you like your coffee?" he asked.

"With cream, but if there isn't any, then I—"

"There is." So they even liked their coffee the same. This could have been damned wonderful. He poured two mugs and handed her one, along with a couple of the cream containers. His hand touched hers, and he immediately felt the effect of that contact in his groin. It wasn't fair that she'd changed the rules like this.

Then again, maybe her change of heart was the best thing that could have happened. She'd been so perfect that she'd scared him. With a woman this terrific, one with no fatal flaws, he was in a danger zone. From the way she was acting now, he didn't have to worry about getting hooked into some long-term deal.

"Want some fruit?" he asked. "It's good."

"No thanks." She pulled out a chair and sat down. "Could you...would you come over here and have a seat, please? I have some things I need to say, and I...I'd like to discuss this like civilized people."

As opposed to jumping each other's bones like uncivilized maniacs. "Sure thing." He abandoned the pear and walked over to sit down at the table, all the while thinking of the meal they'd shared the night before, and how the atmosphere had been charged with sexual tension. It was charged with tension now, but there wasn't anything sexual about it.

Today she wore white shorts and a skinny tank top in mint green—very summery and appealing. Way sexy. Although she wasn't wearing the bangle bracelets, she'd taken time for makeup and a spritz of that cologne he remembered from yesterday.

She looked and smelled a lot like the woman who'd picked him up at the airport, but she sure wasn't acting like her. She ran her red fingernail around the rim of the cup, not bothering to put the cream in that she'd asked for.

He dumped the cream in his, picked up the cup and shook it a little to stir the two together. Then he inhaled the aroma of the coffee and took a bracing sip. He'd grab his thrills where he could get them. "You should try it. Not too bad for in-room coffee."

With a sigh, she opened both cream packets and dumped the contents in simultaneously. Then she stared into the cup, not looking at him. "I didn't know Harry had a twin," she said.

Pausing with his cup halfway to his mouth, he gazed over the rim at her bowed head. *Oh.*

She continued to concentrate on her coffee mug, and her voice was stripped of all emotion. "Stuart and Kim sent me to pick up Harry at the airport. They gave me a picture so I'd recognize him. Turns out Harry got held up with a hospital emergency. He's coming in today."

"You thought I was Harry." A sick feeling lodged in his gut. She hadn't been sent as a special treat by Stuart and Harry. She'd mistaken him for the best man, Stuart's good friend, a respected doctor. That's the person she'd thought she was going to bed with. Damn it. Damn it to hell! Talk about a major blow to the ego. He'd been nothing more than a stand-in for his brother.

She looked up at him, her face flushed. "So when you told me you'd spent the night hauling six people out of a sailboat, I thought—"

"You thought that I was some big *hero?* Jesus." He couldn't look at her, so he stared at the pattern in the Oriental carpet instead. She hadn't bought condoms for a Hollywood stuntman who was something of a playboy. She'd bought them for a twenty-four-carat hero who delivered babies by day and saved the drowning by night. So much for his animal magnetism.

"Is it so hard to believe I'd jump to that conclusion?" She sounded very defensive. "I thought you were Harry! Then you told me that you didn't get any sleep because you spent the night rescuing people from a sailboat, and when I asked you to tell me more, you said you didn't want to talk about it. Maybe if you'd talked about it, I would have figured out it wasn't real!"

He couldn't help but respond to the distress in her voice. Glancing over at her, he discovered what he'd feared, that her eyes were glistening. She was on the verge of tears. He forced out whatever words of comfort he could manage. "I'm sorry we had this big misunderstanding," he said.

"I've never been so humiliated in my life." She swallowed once, twice. Then she picked up her cup, as if determined to drink the coffee if it killed her.

"I don't feel so wonderful about this, myself," he said. "I never pretended to be someone I'm not. I thought I'd met a liberated, sexy woman ready to play, and now I discover it was all a lie. It wasn't me who turned you on, it was some idealized superhero."

She went very still. Slowly she put down the cup and lifted her gaze to meet his. "You have a point. I, um, didn't think of how this might sound to you. I just figured you'd think I was an idiot."

"No bigger one than me," he said carefully. "I was going on my assumptions, too. I didn't want to ask questions, because I liked the way everything was turning out. I thought...I thought maybe Harry and Stuart had asked you to pick me up because they knew we'd get along."

Kate closed her eyes and sighed. "Oh, dear." When she opened her eyes again, her discomfort had been replaced by sympathy. "I'm so sorry. I was so caught up in my own embarrassment that I didn't think about how you'd feel about all this once I told you."

"I'll get over it." The last thing he wanted from her was sympathy.

"Of course you will." A flicker of the energy that had lit her eyes earlier returned. "But I'd be less than honest if I didn't tell you that deluded or not, I had a very ni—"

"Stop right there." Fury burned in his gut. "If you're going to tell me you had a nice time last night, you can save yourself the trouble. There was nothing *nice* about our time together, and you know it." He pinned her with a look intense enough to scorch.

"There was, too!"

"Wrong word, sweetheart. We could hardly wait to get at each other, and once we did, we couldn't get enough. No matter who you thought I was, you can't deny that you were on fire for me. It wasn't *nice*, it was hot as hell. Maybe that was all about me being Mr. Brave and True, but I'm not so sure about that. We had some pure animal lust going on, body to body."

She fidgeted in her chair, as if she'd like to move away, but she didn't, and that little flicker of interest in her eyes grew stronger. She licked her glossy lips. "Maybe."

"No maybe about it." Her reaction made him feel marginally better. And damn, he still wanted her. "The lust isn't gone, either."

"We have to do something about that."

He scooted back his chair. Maybe all wasn't lost, after all. "Come with me, baby. I know exactly what to do about that." If he could reestablish the sexual connection between them, he wouldn't feel like such a fraud.

"No!" She shook her head so vigorously that her short hair quivered. "I mean we have to figure out how to act normal around each other, so that nobody will be able to tell what happened!"

His jaw dropped. "What?"

"I can't let my family know that I picked up the best man's twin by mistake and...and..."

"Why not? Don't people have sex in Rhode Island?"

She stared at him for several long seconds. "Okay, I have an idea."

"I'll bet it's not the same as mine."

A faint smile touched her lips. "No, probably not."

He blew out a breath. "What's the big deal? Through a series of misunderstandings we ended up in bed together. We've both agreed that we had a pretty good time there."

"That's not the point."

Maybe not, but it was a point he really wanted to make. "I'm not proposing to give your family all the gory details, but why can't we laugh about the mix-up and continue to enjoy the weekend together? No harm, no foul. At the end of the weekend we part friends." That would certainly salvage his pride.

She looked at him as if he'd suggested going into the Townsend House breakfast room naked. "You want casual sex." She made it sound like a sacrilege.

"I know that's the term people use, but I never understood it. To me, casual sex is when you don't care very much about whether you do it or not. I love having sex with the right woman, and I try to let her know how much I'm enjoying myself. So, no, I don't want casual sex. I want mind-blowing, incredible, rock-the-bedposts sex, which is what we had." He paused. "And what we could have again."

Although she tried to maintain her expression of outrage, that fire in her eyes burned a little brighter every time he discussed their recent activities. "Well, I...can see that you and I have different ideas on the subject," she said.

He had another thought, one that didn't please him at all. "Are you hoping to get something going with my brother, instead? Is that why you want to make sure we keep our little secret?"

"No, I certainly am not! I don't—"

"Because after spending a very educational night with you, I think I'm qualified to say that you and Harry would be totally unsuited to each other. Don't get me wrong. My brother's a hell of a nice guy. He'll make some sweet girl a good husband."

She bristled. "What's that supposed to mean?"

"Kate, you brought condoms to the room and offered to give me a massage after we'd barely met. Harry wouldn't have the foggiest idea what to do with a firecracker like you."

Cheeks flaming, she pushed away from the table and stood. "I thought you were someone else!"

He leaned back in his chair and gave her a lazy once-over. She had no business looking so good. Later he might regret the remark he was about to make, but now his poor ego needed soothing. "You got what you wanted, didn't you?"

She clenched her fingers, as if restraining the urge to

slap him. Then she opened her mouth, started to say something, and instead remained silent.

He'd give her high marks for honesty, at least. Another woman might have wanted to attack him for pointing out the truth, and then denied the pleasure she'd had out of guilt about the circumstances. Kate obviously felt plenty guilty, but at least she didn't pretend it hadn't been great between them.

"What now?" he asked softly. "You never told me your idea."

"I don't know if it's such a good one, all things considered."

"Hey, let's see if we can be friends, be civilized, like you said. Tell me." He was getting the general impression that Kate was looking for a significant relationship, so he'd have to watch himself with her. She hadn't come right out and said it, but her reaction to his suggestion for the weekend gave her away. There was her fatal flaw, the one he'd been searching for last night.

"Stuart and Harry have quite a few things to take care of today," she said. "Tux rental and stuff, and they're planning to go straight from the airport to Providence so they can make sure everything's handled. They won't be coming down to Newport until late this afternoon, for the rehearsal."

He shrugged. "No problem. I'd figured on that, anyway, and with Harry coming in so late, it makes sense. I can amuse myself."

"They want me to entertain you."

He chuckled and, fortunately, she began to grin, too. If he'd discovered she had no sense of humor about this, he would have been sadly disappointed.

"Don't you have to spend time helping Kim?" he asked.

"Apparently she's talked the two mothers into it. She said Stuart is grateful that you've flown all the way from L.A., and he really wants to make sure you aren't bored and lonely today."

"Oh, Kate, the conversational openings you leave me." He sighed. "But I'm going to prove to you that I can be a gentleman and ignore them. I'm also going to assume you won't be entertaining me in this cottage. So what do you have in mind?"

"A sail."

He couldn't think of anything he'd rather do less than get back in a boat out on the water. But she looked so pleased with herself that he didn't have the heart to say so. "I'd like that."

Her enthusiasm faded immediately. "You don't want to. I can tell by the expression on your face. I should have thought of that, after the filming was so difficult and everything."

"I'd love to go for a sail." He wasn't used to having someone so tuned in to his moods. In less than twenty-four hours they'd become closer than he'd ever been with any other sexual partner. Maybe that was because he and Kate had spent too much time in this cozy setting. Sailing was exactly the kind of outdoor physical activity they needed.

"There are some other things we could do. Maybe you'd rather see one of the lighthouses, or—"

"No, sailing sounds perfect." He was in no mood to tour a lighthouse, as sexually keyed up as he was. He saw them as huge phallic symbols, anyway. "Going out with you today will replace those bad memories of boats with good ones. Let's do it."

She still looked doubtful.

"Really, Kate. I haven't taken a boat out for the fun of it in a long time." He thought of something else to entice her. "You can bring your camera."

"I could, couldn't I?" She brightened. "Are you sure this won't be too much of a busman's holiday for you?"

"Not unless you're planning to wreck us and make me save you."

She seemed skeptical. "Could you really do that? Save me, I mean?"

Her question implied that maybe he couldn't do that. He'd encountered this attitude before. Many people had the idea that because the situations in movies were fake, the stuntmen and women didn't take very big risks, and that they would never manage such feats without help.

The subject was one of his hot buttons, because he thought stuntpeople deserved more respect and recognition than they got. He started to give her the macho answer, one that would tell her in no uncertain terms that he was one bad dude capable of handling any challenge she might dream up.

Then he changed his mind. Thinking that he was a hero had been what had turned her on in the first place, apparently. Perversely, he felt like reversing that image completely. "Probably not," he said. "When it comes to real danger, I'm basically useless."

8

ONCE THEY'D LEFT THE cottage, Kate began to feel better. That extravagant little house—which she'd probably pay for in full because, under the circumstances, she couldn't let Stuart do it—was a constant reminder of her bungle. Technically she could ask Hugh to move into a cheaper room now that she knew he wasn't the best man, but that lacked class. Shelling out her hard-earned cash for that place would be her penance for being such a dope.

But as they walked beside the harbor in the sunshine, she grew more optimistic about how quickly she'd be able to get past this incident. The bustle of wedding activities would begin very soon, and that would force her to shove thoughts of Hugh to the back of her mind. All she had to do was spend a few more hours with him, and she'd be home free. The sailing plan was brilliant, because they'd be too busy working with the boat to get into any more trouble.

She didn't intend to get into any more trouble, regardless of their circumstances, but she'd like to avoid being alone in an enclosed space with him, in case her resolve wasn't all it should be. He might be a swinging California stuntman instead of a heroic Chicago doctor, but he was still a hottie, and he looked way too much like Antonio Banderas.

They grabbed what they decided to call brunch at

an outdoor eatery overlooking the harbor. They both ordered soft-shelled crab sandwiches, and she decided not to make too much of how compatible their eating habits were. It didn't matter. On Sunday he'd go back to L.A. and that would be that.

The good meal in cheerful surroundings improved her mood even more. She'd always been invigorated by the sight of sailboats scudding along in the breeze. There was something so decadent and carefree about sailboats—they had the same panache as a convertible. From her seat at the table she had a panoramic view of bright boats with sails in every color of the rainbow.

For the time being, she kept her camera in her purse. Much as she hated to admit it, she was fascinated by Hugh and didn't feel like taking pictures of her surroundings. Now that she knew what he did for a living, she couldn't resist asking him about the Hollywood stars he'd worked with.

Besides the tales of her Grandpa Charlie's heroism, she'd fed her dramatic soul with movies, and for a while had even dreamed of being an actress. But photography was the family business, and she'd been attracted to the idea of following in her father's footsteps and taking over the studio in partnership with Kim. She had the uncomfortable thought that despite claiming a thirst for adventure, she hadn't taken many authentic risks.

Hugh had taken hundreds, shooting on location in all kinds of exotic places. She started thinking of him as her faux hero, a guy with all the trappings and none of the substance. Being with him reminded her of binging on junk food. You knew it wasn't good for you, but for instant gratification it couldn't be beat.

They found a place within walking distance that rented small sailboats and they happened to have one left. Kate was a decent sailor, but when Hugh said he could handle the boat, she decided to sit back and let him do it so she could take pictures. Some time later, after he'd successfully navigated out of the harbor and around the Castle Hill Lighthouse into Rhode Island Sound, she grudgingly had to admit he knew what he was doing.

She also had to admit that she was having a good time. The wind carried them along at a good clip, which was how she liked it. At this speed the boat heeled sharply to starboard, so she did her job as the crew and hung on to the port side to help balance. Flying along like this reminded her of driving her Miata, except that here she had the rhythmic slap of the waves and the occasional spray of saltwater to make the experience even more invigorating. Gulls wheeled overhead and people from nearby boats waved in greeting.

Kate couldn't help being proud that she was out here with someone who looked like Hugh. Faux hero or not, he made a damned fine sight sitting in the stern of the boat, his capable hand on the tiller, the wind ruffling his dark hair, the sun glinting off his aviator shades. They'd both worn the bulky orange life jackets issued to them in the beginning, but after leaving the harbor they'd both agreed to shuck them for the duration. The Coast Guard wouldn't like it if they got caught, but the darned jackets were hot.

So there he was, the wind molding his T-shirt to his muscled chest and making him look sexier than ever. She took an entire roll of film, and a good part of it included him. She wondered if she'd go see the movie he'd been shooting before he came here. Might not be wise.

He'd followed her lead and worn shorts today, which gave her a nice view of his solid calves and strong thighs. Every time she glanced at his knees, though, she remembered how he'd balanced her there while they were in the tub. When he changed his grip on the tiller, she thought of the way he'd touched her in so many creative ways. His smile brought memories of his kiss.

How naive she'd been to imagine that when they'd kissed, he would know he'd found his soul mate. All he'd found was a hot little companion for the weekend. In his tales of Hollywood, he'd painted a picture of a life where relationships were intense and fleeting. No wonder he'd been so delighted to find her waiting for him in the airport. She must have seemed like the perfect candidate for a weekend fling.

"This is great!" he called above the steady slap of the waves. "You were right, I wasn't crazy about this idea at first, but there's a huge difference between sailing your own boat on a sunny day and swimming back and forth in cold water from one boat to the other, in the dark, lugging deadweight."

"You're a good sailor," she said.

He smiled, showing off those beautiful teeth that had nipped gently at her skin. "Thanks. So are you."

"Do you sail a lot in California?"

"Whenever I can. I took lessons a few years ago. Every skill I pick up makes me more marketable as a stuntman. I know a little bit about a lot of things."

And a lot about making love. "So you do the kind of stuff the actors either can't or won't," she said.

"That's about the size of it."

She knew some actors used body doubles for nude scenes. "Have you ever been a stand-in for someone who didn't want to take his clothes off?" The question popped out, and the minute it did, she knew she'd made a mistake.

"Yes."

"Oh." She was *not* going to ask him which movie.

He told her anyway, and it was a film she'd seen, one she'd be able to rent anytime she wanted. She vowed that she'd never watch it again. Never. Of course not. Well, maybe once.

Hugh gazed at her. "That was an interesting question."

"I can't imagine why I even asked it."

"I can." He paused. "You've never had sex just for the hell of it, have you?"

She hesitated. If she said yes, she'd be lying, but if she said no, she'd look like little miss provincial, a girl who didn't have the courage to have the kind of *Sex in the City* life that urban professional women were supposed to have these days. She'd already acted prudish by accusing him of wanting casual sex. In today's world, there was nothing wrong with that.

"I'll take your silence as a no," he said. "It's okay. We need to understand each other, that's all. You don't have sex for the hell of it, and that's the only reason I do have it. We can't get confused about that."

"Don't worry. I won't."

"I only bring it up because I can tell you're still thinking about the sex we had."

"I am not!" Which of course she was, whether she intended to or not, and that's why she'd accidentally asked him about the nude scene.

"Are so."

"What an ego!" She felt as if he'd backed her into a corner, and she came out swinging. "I am *so* not thinking of having sex with you!" She forgot how sound carried across the water.

A sleek racing sailboat passed them, and a guy in the boat made a megaphone of his hands. "Hey, go ahead!" the guy yelled. "It's a beautiful day, and life's too short!"

Kate flushed, but she was on a roll and the devil had control of her tongue. "Well, so's his schnitzel!" she yelled back.

Hugh's bark of astonished laughter made her glance over at him. She shrugged, trying to pretend nonchalance. "Just having a little fun."

"Oh, no, you don't." He pitched his voice low enough that only she could hear him. "You don't get to play those games and get away with it."

"You started it."

"No, I most certainly did not. Not now, and not yesterday. Watch your head. We're coming about." He pointed the boat toward shore.

She dodged the swinging boom and moved to the starboard side of the boat. "What—what are you doing?"

"Finding a quiet place where we can talk."

"Um, that's okay." She couldn't decide if the squiggles of sensation in her tummy were panic or excitement. Maybe a little of both. "I probably shouldn't have said that."

"Probably not."

"Let's just keep going." She tucked her camera back in her purse and stashed it under the hull. Now was not the time to be taking pictures.

"Let's not. I talk better when I don't have to worry about navigating."

"But we don't have anything to talk about." She'd made a mistake letting him take charge of this boat, but there wasn't much she could about it now.

Well, she could grovel. "Okay, you're right! I'm having a tough time forgetting about last night, probably because I don't do the casual sex thing. But I promise not to bring up a single charged topic of conversation again. I shouldn't have asked you about the nude scene. That was uncalled for."

He didn't respond, just kept tacking the boat toward shore.

"And I shouldn't have yelled out a comment—an *untrue* comment, I might add—about the size of your, um... Anyway, I shouldn't have done that, either. Sometimes I get carried away."

"Uh-huh."

"Hugh, you can't just beach this sucker, you know. There're cliffs, and rocks, and you said you were no good at saving us if we wreck, so why don't we keep going?"

Smiling serenely at her, he continued on course toward shallow water.

As they glided in, she peered over the side. "Yikes, there're boulders under there, Hugh. Big boulders."

"I know. That's why we're going to tie up to that buoy ahead. Lower the sails, Kate."

"Why would you want to tie up?" She had an inkling, though. She was in trouble.

"I have my reasons."

She'd bet he did, and they had to do with teaching her a lesson. But she didn't want to make things worse by arguing with him and possibly causing them to run up on something, so she lowered the sails. As he guided them toward the red and white buoy bobbing in the water ahead, she leaned over the prow with a line.

When the buoy came within reach, she grabbed the metal ring on top and secured the boat. She doubted the owner of the buoy would mind. It probably belonged to a lobster fisherman who wouldn't come out to check his lobster pots until later in the day. Once they were moored, she turned to discover that Hugh had tied the boom out of the way and was sitting on the starboard side of the boat, watching her.

She swallowed a lump of nervousness. "Now what?"

He gestured to the bench along the port side. "Have a seat."

She sat down facing him as the boat rocked gently on the waves. By moving closer to shore, he'd isolated them more than a little. And since there was no beach tucked into the rocks here, no one would have reason to come near the rocky cliff beside them.

Farther out on the water they'd been surrounded by power boats, yachts and smaller sailboats like this one. Now all that traffic skimmed by in the distance. The roar of outboard and inboard motors was muted here.

She was within arm's reach of Hugh, but he didn't try to grab her. Instead he sat with his forearms braced on his thighs, his hands hanging loosely between his knees. He was easily the most handsome, sexy man she'd ever shared a sailboat with. Or a sports car. Or a whirlpool. Or a king-size bed.

He gazed at her. "I hope you know I want to strip you naked right this minute."

She gulped and laced her fingers together, gripping them hard as her pulse raced out of control.

"But I won't. I didn't bring any of your condoms along, for one thing."

"And I'd scream my head off, for another thing."

His smile was almost predatory. "I know you would...eventually. You do get loud about it, which is something I happen to enjoy. But out here on the water, as we've just seen, sound carries, and I wouldn't want to bring unwanted visitors down on us."

So he wasn't planning to seduce her. She was relieved, of course. Definitely relieved. Right. So relieved.

"You should see the color in your cheeks. I'm betting you're secretly sorry I didn't tuck a couple of those little raincoats in my pocket."

"No, I'm—"

"Never mind. It's just that you always look so damned sexy that I keep getting sidetracked." He paused and cleared his throat. "But I have some questions for you, and the first one is, where in the hell did you get the term *schnitzel?*"

Her heart beat faster. "Oh, that."

"Yeah, that."

"Kim and I came up with it. We had a few code words we used mostly in front of our mom, so she wouldn't know we were checking out guys. I haven't thought of that word in years and, in the heat of the moment, it slipped out. I'm surprised I even remembered it, to be honest."

"To be honest," he repeated. "Do you really want to be honest?"

She wasn't sure. Up to now she'd always tried, but total honesty with this guy could sink her, but good.

"I can see that's a hard question," he said. "So I'll go first, because I like the concept of honesty. I like it a whole lot."

"Me, too, but—"

"But you're scared to death, right? You have urges you can't control, and that's not a comfy feeling, is it?"

Yes, she had urges. Like right now, as he sat with his knees apart, she could see the considerable bulge rounding out the seam of his crotch. In hers and Kim's teenage world that would have called for a major schnitzel alert. "If I'd known who you were from the beginning, none of this would be happening," she said.

"So you're sorry about last night?"

She took a deep breath. "No."

"Well, that's something, at least. Because I can guarantee you that I'm not sorry. If it took a twin mix-up for you to strip down and jump into bed with me, I'm delighted you thought I was Harry. But now that you know I'm the evil twin Hugh, I'm wondering if either of us can put all that chemistry back in the bottle."

"I'm going to try my damnedest." She didn't know if her damnedest would be enough. She was discovering something shocking about herself. Last night she'd had sex with this man because she believed he was a hero and quite possibly her soul mate.

Today she knew he was neither of those things, and she wanted to have sex with him, anyway. The memory of the pleasure he'd given her was permanently etched in her mind, and it would take only the barest of touches to ignite the blaze once again. The rocking of the boat and the soft slap of the water against the hull seemed almost sexual, but then everything seemed sexual at that moment.

"What's the point in fighting it?" he asked gently.

Her body turned to maple syrup when he used that tone of voice. "Look, it would be easy for you to say that. Sunday you'll fly back to L.A. I'll be the one left to deal with the teasing and innuendoes. I mean, if they ever found out that I went to bed with you without having the slightest idea who you are..."

"They don't ever have to know that."

"But they could suspect it, if we're too friendly with each other when we're together. You know how people jump to conclusions."

"I know." His breathing was steady, but now his hands were clenched together, so he wasn't quite as relaxed as he might want to appear. "But they don't have to jump that far. Did you tell Kim where you were when you called her back?"

"No."

"There you have it. Just imply that you dropped me at the inn, thinking I was Harry, but when you came down this morning to spend the day with me, you knew exactly who I was. So we're attracted to each other. Is that a crime?"

"Let me think a minute."

He leaned back, propping his elbows against the boat. "Take your time. But not too much. It'll take us a while to sail back and get those condoms."

She decided the sunlight and sea air must be messing with her head, because she was beginning to see the sense in his logic. Why shouldn't a twenty-six-year-old, unattached woman enjoy herself with the handsome stranger from the West Coast? Where was it written that every sexual experience had to lead into a long-term relationship with someone she might eventually marry?

Come to think of it, she'd never really expected to marry anybody she'd been sexually involved with in the past. Oh, she'd tried to pretend it was love, and that those men would somehow morph into the kind of hero and soul mate she required, but deep in her heart she'd known they'd never make the grade.

Hugh was suggesting that the two of them continue what they'd started, and now that she'd experienced sex with him she was sorely tempted to experience it again. And again. If she was denying herself because of what other people might think, then she needed to grow up and get over that. She wasn't worried about her reputation when she thought they were star-crossed lovers, so why not be that brave now, when she was only after some really amazing sex?

However, if she doubted that she could tell him goodbye on Sunday without remorse and regrets, then that was a legitimate reason for saying no. Or was it? She might as well face the truth—she'd never taken a certified risk in her life. Here was her chance.

She'd go into it knowing he'd be looking for a new chickie-babe on the other side of the country once this adventure was over. She would be a notch in his belt but, viewing it another way, he'd be a notch in hers. He would be her first thrilling, terrifying, heart-stopping risk.

She cleared her throat. "If we agree to be, um—"

"Lovers?" he suggested helpfully.

She really wanted him. Really, really. "If we do, then you have to promise me that you won't discuss that with anyone. If they pick up on it, that's fine, but—"

"Whoa, *whoa.*" He sat up straight. "I think I've just been insulted."

"I'm only asking you to be discreet."

"I'm going to forgive the insult because you think you don't know much about me, considering how little time we've spent together. But you know me better than you think. A man says a lot about himself during sex."

She couldn't think too hard about that or she was liable to leap over there and start unzipping his shorts. "Well, of course, you were very...very considerate, and obliging, and..." And *hot.*

"I treated you with respect. A man who respects the woman he's involved with doesn't go around discussing their mutual sexual activities with other people. Locker-room talk is for immature little boys. Don't put me in that category."

Oh, she certainly would not. As he sat across from her, his shoulders looking as broad as the whole darned boat, she would put him in the all-man, all-the-time category. "I'm sorry. You're right. I should have known not to imply that you'd gossip about us."

"I'll do better than that. I'll protect you from gossip as much as I can." He leaned forward. "Are you telling me that you're interested?"

Her heart rate picked up. "My first obligation is to Kim. I couldn't ever let myself get so distracted that I let her down in any way."

"Goes without saying."

"When the weekend's over, so are we."

"Understood."

She took a shaky breath. "Then...yes."

He sat very still, and if she hadn't seen a muscle in

his jaw twitch, she would have thought he was totally unaffected by her answer.

Then he let out his breath in one long, controlled sigh. "God, I was afraid you were going to say no, and that would make this one of the most miserable weekends of my life."

"Really?" She looked at him in surprise. "It's only one weekend. I'm only one woman out of—how many?" Those were the kinds of things she'd keep reminding herself. He made love like an angel because he was a devil with women.

"That's not important. Right now, for this weekend, you're the only woman in the world, and I want you so bad I'm going crazy." He grinned. "My schnitzel's going crazy."

She laughed. "Then I guess we'd better get back to the cottage and get some protection for your schnitzel."

"The sooner the better. We'll get the sails up and—" Then he paused and glanced around. "Did you happen to notice something?"

"Like what?"

"Like the breeze is totally...gone."

9

"OMIGOD, YOU'RE RIGHT," Kate said.

Hugh surveyed the boats out on the Sound. "The water's smooth as glass clear to the horizon. Not a whitecap anywhere. The only folks moving out there are using motors."

"We have a motor."

Hugh glanced at the small outboard attached to the stern. "I was hoping we wouldn't have to depend on it. It didn't sound too healthy when we used it to get out past the breakwater."

"They never sound healthy. It'll probably do the job."

"Let's hope." He moved to the stern and took hold of the starter. "Keep your fingers crossed." He yanked hard on the cord. The motor growled softly and stopped. He yanked again and got a slightly louder growl that went nowhere. Several more tries produced the same result.

"Want me to try?"

His macho reaction was to say, hell, no, that if anyone could get the thing started, he could, and this motor was obviously D.O.A. But he didn't want to get into a power struggle with Kate at the very moment she'd agreed to be his playmate for the weekend. "Be my guest." He traded seats with her.

She tried a few times, and he felt a little smug that

she couldn't do it, either. "Maybe you should try again," she said.

They traded seats once more and he nearly pulled the cord out of the socket, but the motor refused to start.

Kate sighed and looked at the oars tucked along the inside of the hull. "We could row," she said without enthusiasm.

Hugh hated to think about how long it would take him to paddle this tub back to the harbor. "We could."

"Or I could get out my cell phone and call the Coast Guard." She held his gaze, a smile teasing her mouth.

"I'd rather row." He knew what happened when the Coast Guard showed up. They lashed you to their seriously important boat and towed you, their twirling blue lights announcing that they'd rescued yet another Sunday sailor who thought he was going for the America's Cup. It wasn't an image Hugh wanted to carry away from this weekend.

"I didn't think you'd go for that," she said.

"No, but that does narrow our options." He didn't relish the idea of rowing, but if that was the only way he'd get Kate in bed with him again, he'd row his little heart out.

He reached for the oar tucked along the starboard side. "If you'll untie us, I'll take the first shift." He had no intention of letting her row, but having seen her independent streak, he wanted to let her think that he would.

"Or..."

Something in her tone made him glance up.

She was leaning against the rail in a suggestive pose, her nipples puckering the lime sherbet knit of her top. "Or we could find something to do until the breeze picks up," she said in as sultry a voice as any Hollywood starlet had ever managed.

The oar dropped from his suddenly lax fingers and clattered to the floor of the boat. He could imagine a few scenarios, but he wanted to know if she was on the same page. He took off his sunglasses and put them on the seat beside him. Then he leaned toward her. "We could. What do you have in mind?"

"A little mutual satisfaction."

He was instantly hard and his pulse jumped crazily. "Noise carries across the water," he reminded her.

She ran a tongue over her lips. "So don't make any."

He burned for her. She might not realize it, but she was clearly getting into this forbidden affair business, finally letting herself enjoy the concept. That gave an already dynamite woman the equivalent of nuclear power.

He cleared his throat. "I can control myself. It's you we have to worry about."

"Let's test that and see." She pushed herself up from the bench, and in one smooth movement lowered herself to her knees right between his open thighs. Slowly she took off her sunglasses and laid them on the seat beside his. Her green eyes glittered with excitement. "Ready to show me how quietly you can come?"

He couldn't breathe. "You mean, you're just going to..."

"Why not?" She slid her finger under the cloth flap covering his zipper and ran her knuckle up and down the metal track. "You can keep watch and let me know if any boats meander in this direction." She tucked her tongue in the corner of her mouth and gave him that look that drove him wild. "Unless you're afraid to take a chance."

He groaned. "When you decide to be bad, you really max out."

"I don't believe in moderation." She eased the zipper down as she gazed into his eyes. "Do you?"

Totally mesmerized by her, he shook his head.

Her smile tantalized him with the promise of those full lips. "I didn't think so."

She was magnificent, and he'd really dug himself into a hole this time. Minutes ago he'd been determined to talk her into continuing their affair because he couldn't imagine how he'd make it through the weekend without having sex with her again. She'd agreed to his proposal—a brief, intense relationship that would end on Sunday. That agreement eliminated her only fatal flaw, which left him wide open. He could so easily fall for her under these circumstances. Obviously he'd been thinking with his schnitzel.

But there was no going back. He couldn't imagine any man having the strength to call a halt when a woman like Kate was on her knees in front of him, freeing his stiff penis from his briefs. This kind of seduction was every man's fantasy, and he was helpless to stop her. He'd pay his dues later.

But right now...ahhh. Right now she held him firmly with her slender fingers and covered him with lollipop licks. He cupped her head in both hands and moaned.

"Nice?"

"Mmm."

"Watch for boats," she whispered, her breath cool against his moist skin.

Yeah, right. Like he'd be able to tear his attention away from the sight of her face in his lap, her pink lips nuzzling the most needy part of him.

"Watching?" she murmured.

"Mmm. *Mmm.*" Hell, nobody could creep up on them anyway. They'd have to use a motor and he'd hear that. At least he hoped he would. "I'm..." He gasped as she slid her mouth halfway down his penis and did some number with her tongue at the same time. "I'm...listening."

That could be a huge lie. What she was doing with her tongue was pretty much making him deaf. The blood was roaring in his ears and his heart was beating so loudly it was probably scaring the fish swimming by.

He spread his arms and gripped the rail behind him as he concentrated on not groaning. Although he made his living in the performing arts, he had no intention of letting the world witness this particular performance.

Also, because he was supposed to be this worldly type from the jaded streets of Hollywood, he didn't want to seem too easy, too susceptible to what she was doing. He failed miserably. Her clever caress made him whimper like a puppy.

He couldn't watch anymore, because that alone was threatening to finish him off. Throwing his head back, he clenched his jaw and tried to hold off the orgasm she was building towards. But when she flicked her tongue like *that*, and applied pressure like *that*, then he....

Oh, damn, there it was, the point of no return. He couldn't stop this. Couldn't stop—with a cry that he only partly succeeded in swallowing, he erupted into her mouth.

Delirious with pleasure, he quivered and panted as she drained him of every drop. No, she didn't believe in moderation. When she offered a guy oral sex, she gave him a top-of-the-line experience. He lay slumped against the side of the boat, gradually adjusting to reality, eyes still closed, as she tenderly tucked him back inside his shorts and zipped the fly.

Slowly he opened his eyes and found her sitting back on her heels watching him, a satisfied smile on her face. He smiled back as the boat rocked them gently. Moments this good should be enjoyed, not analyzed, and he'd always been a master at staying in the present.

But this time something new happened. As he gazed at her, he began to wonder how he'd manage to stumble through his future days when he could no longer look into those bright eyes. This was crazy. He'd known her for a mere twenty-four hours. She couldn't have become that important to him so soon.

"I don't think you were a very good sentinel," she said.

"I was a terrible sentinel." He began to imagine all the wonderful things he could do to make her quiver as he had.

"You made noise."

"Yeah." He sat forward and took her by the shoulders. "Because you pushed me past my limit. And now let's see if you—"

"Wait, did you feel that?"

"What?"

"The wind."

"What about it?" A little wind wouldn't stop him from driving her straight out of her mind.

The breeze ruffled her hair as she pointed toward the collapsed sails. "You know, the *wind*."

"Oh. The *wind*." He released her and checked the horizon. Sure enough, folks were sailing briskly along, and the smooth water had become choppy again. His brain must have gone into complete meltdown during that last episode. He'd totally forgotten why they were still anchored here instead of headed back to the Townsend House and an innerspring mattress.

"We should go back. In case the wind dies again."

He had to agree, especially since he hadn't been looking forward to rowing home. But he couldn't resist teasing her. "You're just afraid you won't do any better than I did at watching for boats and keeping quiet."

She arched her eyebrows. "Is that a challenge?"

"Maybe it is." He wondered how fast he could make it happen for her. It might be worth tackling that long row home to win a very erotic game.

Her eyes flashed and her chin lifted. "What do you plan to do about it?"

"Prove my point." Coordination was one of his strong suits, and he had her shorts unbuttoned and pushed to her knees before she realized what he'd planned to do.

"Hugh!"

"This'll only take a few minutes." That was a pretty large boast, but he thought he could back it up.

"But—"

"Go with it." Bracing his feet apart so he wouldn't capsize them, he lifted her up onto the prow of the boat. Her shorts dropped neatly to the floor. "Have fun."

"I don't know if this is a good—"

"Hang on to the mast. And watch for boats." As he stretched the elastic leg opening of her lace panties and sank to his knees, the sweet aroma of aroused woman greeted him, and he congratulated himself on doing exactly the right thing. A gentleman didn't take his pleasure and leave his lady in the lurch.

Another time he would have lingered over this delectable prospect, but with the wind picking up, someone might sail near enough to spy on them if he didn't make this quick. He ran his tongue over her once, tasting and enjoying. Her quick intake of breath was his reward.

But he had a bigger reward in mind. Settling in, he concentrated all his efforts on that magic spot that should have her quivering in no time. Sure enough, it did. Her moans were muffled, as if she'd clamped her mouth closed, but she was pretty darned noisy, too.

Then he hit the mother lode and she nearly fell off the prow of the boat as she bucked in the grip of her orgasm. The boat rocked wildly, and he grabbed her and held on while he put the finishing touches on his erotic artwork.

She was gasping as frantically as he had by the time he lifted his mouth and pulled her damp panties back in place. And for the record, she'd also cried out, louder than he had. He loved knowing that he'd made her forget everything except the pleasure he was giving her.

Standing carefully, he eased her back to the bench. Then he made the mistake of looking into her eyes. He expected them to be glazed with satisfaction, and they were. But beneath that sensual daze lurked a vulnerability that put a hammerlock on his heart.

He was in so much trouble.

DURING THE SAIL BACK TO the harbor, Kate lifted her face to the wind in giddy delight. This feeling of sexual abandon was so cool. Maybe Hugh wasn't the kind of hero she'd had in mind, but he had the sense of adventure she'd always craved in a man. With him leading the way, she could dare all kinds of things, including sex in a sailboat.

But now they needed to make tracks for that little cottage behind the inn. With luck they might steal an hour alone before heading to the wedding rehearsal at Belcourt Castle. At one time the prospect of spending time in a place like Belcourt would have thrilled her dramatic little heart. At the moment it was merely a nuisance that would interfere with making love to Hugh. She'd have to work hard to stay focused on Kim's wedding, but somehow she'd have to do that.

While Hugh tacked this way and that trying to catch the best wind, Kate did her part by lending her weight to whichever side of the boat needed balancing. They worked smoothly together, saying little, as if their shared goal of getting back to their private hideaway had molded them into one efficient unit. Yet the afternoon had begun to slip away as they docked at the marina and Hugh settled the bill with the rental company.

Kate glanced at her watch as they left the marina. "The rehearsal's in less than an hour." She could feel the wedding closing in on them, destroying the intimacy they'd had. Being wild and free when she was alone with Hugh was one thing, but carrying off the same emotion when surrounded by her family was a different challenge.

"That doesn't give us much time." Hugh took her hand as they walked quickly along the crowded sidewalk on their way back to the Townsend House.

Instinctively she pulled her hand out of his grasp.

"Hey." He stopped walking.

Pausing to look over her shoulder at him, she wondered if she'd hurt his feelings. "I'm sorry. It's just that we're in public now, and I—"

"Well, what do you know." His gaze flicked over her.

"What?"

"There's a big yellow streak running right down the back of that skinny little top and white shorts of yours. I didn't notice it before."

She spun to face him. "I'm not a coward!" *Or was she?* "I thought we agreed that we wouldn't parade our relationship in front of people."

Although his eyes were covered by his sunglasses, the tightening of his jaw signaled his reaction. "I have no intention of doing that. I always thought holding hands meant you were very interested in someone, but unless the code is different in Rhode Island, I don't think it's the same as announcing that I'm sleeping with you."

She flushed, irritated with herself. "You're right, it doesn't. I...I guess I overreacted."

He stepped closer and lowered his voice. "And maybe that decision you made out on the water isn't the right one, after all."

She felt like such a little hick. Some free spirit she was, if she couldn't handle a weekend fling without getting paranoid. Taking a deep breath, she ignored the curious glances coming their way and held out her hand. "It was the right decision. Please forgive me for acting like a jerk."

He hesitated.

"I won't freak out on you again," she said. "I promise."

Slowly he reached for her hand and laced his fingers through hers. Then he pulled her into his arms. He held her in a loose grip, allowing her to move away easily if that's what she wanted to do.

She figured he might be testing her, so she smiled and slid her arms around his neck.

"How does this feel?" he asked.

"Fine." Her heart rate sped up.

"You're sure? Remember we're gonna be honest with each other."

She looked up at him, her attention drawn to his mouth, the mouth that had so recently given her a wonderful orgasm. The longer they stayed like this, the more aware she became of his body brushing against hers. He was starting to get aroused, and so was she. She'd never experienced that kind of intensity in the middle of a public thoroughfare.

"Kate?" he prompted.

"Well, I'm a little nervous, okay?"

"I thought so."

"When I'm this close to you I feel as if I'm giving off sparks, and I wonder if anybody can see them."

"And what if they did? Don't tell me you've never embraced a guy in public before."

"Not a guy like you."

He chuckled. "I'm not sure what that means."

"It means—" She paused to swallow. "It means that my other boyfriends have been...safe."

"And I'm not?"

"No, you're definitely not safe. But the thing is, I've decided to live dangerously this weekend. Take risks."

A hint of a smile touched his lips. "Me, too."

"You do that all the time."

"Yeah, but not..." He gazed at her. Then he shrugged. "I guess a risk is a risk. So, do you want to practice not freaking out?"

Her anxiety rose a notch. "In what way?"

"These are strangers. Let's see if you can handle a little kiss in front of strangers."

She'd never been able to turn down a dare, and this was definitely a dare. "Okay, let's see."

He lowered his head. "Let's see."

In comparison to the lust-filled kisses they'd shared in the past few hours, this one was fairly restrained. But Kate was discovering that no kiss from this man could be labeled tame. The pressure of his mouth reminded her of every erotic moment they'd experienced, and the soft glide of his tongue made her want to rip his clothes off so that they could experience a few more.

When he lifted his head again, her breathing was ragged and she was clutching his shoulders hard enough to make her fingers cramp.

"We'd better get back," he murmured.

She nodded. "I want to live dangerously, but I'd rather not get arrested."

Then a very familiar voice called her name. The tone was all too familiar, too. It usually meant she was in big trouble.

Kate turned her head to see her mother standing about ten feet away, gaping at her. And there was her father, looking equally amazed.

Busted.

10

THE FAMILY RESEMBLANCE was strong enough for Hugh to figure out that these attractive fifty-somethings were Kate's parents, even before she hastily pulled away from him and greeted them as Mom and Dad. Through the stumbling introductions on Kate's part and the handshakes on his, Hugh took stock of the people who had produced such an amazing daughter.

Her father was the one who'd passed on the red hair. His was darker and flecked with gray, but no doubt it used to be the color of Kate's. He was dressed casually, in a knit polo shirt and slacks, but his expression was anything but relaxed. His mouth was set in a firm line, as if he wanted to demand Hugh's intentions.

Hugh didn't blame him. Most fathers wouldn't be happy to see their daughter in the arms of a guy they'd never met, and John Cooper didn't know the half of it.

Kate's mother, Emily, a trim brunette in a red silk pants suit, wasn't smiling, either. But Hugh had hope that she might, eventually. The laugh lines around her mouth promised a sense of humor lurked in there somewhere, and meeting on the sidewalk like this was right out of a sitcom.

Still, he regretted making things awkward for Kate.

Hell, he regretted making things awkward for himself. He hadn't met a girlfriend's parents since high school. All the women he'd been involved with had known in advance he wasn't the guy they'd take home to meet the folks.

"We've been, uh, sailing." Kate glanced at her watch. "And you know what? I think we'd all better get back to the Townsend House. It'll be time for the rehearsal before you know it."

"Now that's a switch," Emily said. "You worrying about whether we're late or not. Anyway, I don't think we have to rush. Your dad and I wondered where you were, and then we saw your car in the Townsend House parking lot so we decided to come and look for you."

"You could have tried my cell phone," Kate said. Then she flinched, as if realizing that sounded too much like *you should have called first.* "What I mean is, that's a great way to—"

"I hate those damn things," her father said. "Anyway, we found you without having to resort to that."

They'd come specifically to get a look at him, Hugh decided. Kim had relayed Kate's anxiety about the mix-up and, following their parental instincts, they'd decided something unusual was going on. They'd been dead-on.

Kate's father focused his laserlike gaze on Hugh. "Stuart told me you're in the movie business out in L.A."

Hugh picked up on the subtext right away. *You live clear across the country, so why are you putting a lip lock on a Rhode Island girl?* "I have a condo in L.A., but I'm hardly ever there," he said. "I do a lot of shooting on location. There's a movie I'll be doing down in Virginia next fall." And why he'd said that, he had no idea.

"Sounds like an interesting life," Kate's mother said. "A little on the vagabond side, though. All that traveling must get tiring after a while."

"Sometimes." *More each year.* He hadn't acknowledged to himself just how much the travel was bothering him lately, because then he'd have to question his whole lifestyle.

"Well!" Kate said. "I don't know about anybody else, but I need to get back to my room and change."

"Go ahead, dear, if you feel you need to." Emily continued to gaze at Hugh, obviously not finished with him yet.

Hugh understood that Kate was trying to break up this little interview, but he doubted she'd leave him here alone with her parents. Her father continued to glare at him, but Hugh understood. If Hugh had a daughter, he'd glare at a guy like him, too.

"Our son, Nick, travels around a lot, too," Emily said. "He's a foreign correspondent, which gives him a chance to indulge his hobby of photographing exotic places. We hardly ever get to see him, except at events like this. I keep wishing he'd settle down, but so far he's shown no sign of it." Apparently Emily wasn't as territorial as her husband, although she didn't like that her son was a rolling stone, and probably wouldn't want her daughter mixed up with one, either.

She didn't have to worry about Kate getting mixed up with him, but he didn't think she'd be thrilled about the weekend affair, either. "So you have a whole family of photographers," he said.

Kate's mother smiled for the first time. "Except for me. I teach belly dancing."

"No kidding?"

Kate gave her mother an affectionate glance. "No kidding. She's great, too."

"I'll bet." Hugh was charmed. Kate might have inherited red hair and a talent for photography from her father, but her sense of adventure came straight from her mom. He could get along with Emily, not that he would ever have to test that.

John Cooper was a different story. "How soon are you going back to California?" he asked, his tone implying that it couldn't be soon enough for him.

"Sunday afternoon." He could see himself reflected in John's sunglasses and had to admit he looked exactly like what he was—a good-time guy on the make. "How about you two?"

"We're staying on a few days," John said. "I thought Kate might be able to use my help at the studio. She and Kim have taken quite a bit of time off in the past few weeks."

And you aren't helping matters, stud. Hugh heard the unspoken message loud and clear. No, John Cooper didn't have much use for him.

"That would be great, Dad." Kate smiled at him. Then she sent Hugh a pleading glance. "You know, I really think we'd better go back and get ready. I'm not walking into Belcourt Castle looking like this."

Hugh thought she looked fantastic, all windblown, healthy and well kissed. They'd wasted so much time since leaving the marina that there was no chance he'd be able to take her to bed, though. She might not be willing, anyway, now that they'd run into her parents like this. The whole program might be jeopardized.

At any rate, he was sure she wanted to shower, put on fresh clothes and try to regain her equilibrium. "I need to get changed, too," he said. "Let's head back."

"You two go on, then," Emily said. "We don't have to change clothes and, as lovely as the Townsend House is, I'd rather stay out here and watch the boats, wouldn't you, John?"

"I don't know, Em. Maybe we should see if Kim and Stuart are—"

"John."

"Right. Kim and Stuart are handling everything just fine. We'll stay out here and watch the boats."

Hugh grinned. Maybe ol' John wasn't so intimidating after all if his wife could rein him in that easily. "Then I guess we'll see you both at the rehearsal."

"Why don't you ride over there with us?" Emily asked.

Kate looked quickly at Hugh. "I don't know if—"

"Sure," Hugh said. His hat was off to Emily Cooper. She didn't trust him any more than her husband did, obviously. And he'd bet the keys to his Corvette that she'd decided to spend every spare moment this weekend keeping an eye on him. He'd let her do that. She had to sleep sometime.

EMILY WATCHED HER daughter and the stuntman walk away. She had a premonition about this one. Up to now, Kate hadn't met anyone with her level of energy. Hugh Armstrong crackled with energy.

"He's trouble," John said. "I'm going to have a chat with Stuart. I think he set Kate up with a Romeo, and I don't like it one damned bit."

"John, don't you dare say a word. Don't interfere."

Her husband turned to her in amazement. "Don't

interfere? You're one to talk! I seem to remember several times when you—"

"Moving to Florida gave me some perspective," she said. "Besides that, Kim managed to find Stuart when I wasn't even in the same state, so I'm starting to believe in letting nature take its course."

"Em, the guy's a playboy! Anybody with two eyes can see that!"

Emily took his arm and guided him down the sidewalk, away from the direction of the Townsend House. "Keep your voice down, darling. They're not out of sight yet."

"I don't care if he hears me," her husband grumbled, but he lowered the volume. "He's from Hollywood, for Chrissake. You know the kind of thing that goes on out there. He's going to dazzle Kate for the weekend and then take off, never to be heard from again."

"I don't think so. Did you see the way he looked at her?"

"I certainly did, and I was ready to punch him out."

"John, he's smitten."

"Ha. Look, the guy's thirty-five, same as Harry, and he's never even been engaged, according to Stuart. Doesn't that tell you something?"

Emily smiled. "Uh-huh. It tells me he's ripe for the picking."

HEART POUNDING, Kate lengthened her stride as she headed for the Townsend House. "The deal's off."

"I was afraid of that."

"So I'm a coward." She took a shaky breath. One run-in with her parents and she folded. She wasn't thrilled to discover her limits, but there they were.

"I'm not the kind of girl you're used to out in California," she said. "The fact is, I can't carry on an affair with you right under my parents' noses."

"Kate, I'm really sorry about what just happened. Believe me, if I'd had any idea they'd show up, I wouldn't have kissed you."

She glanced at him, surprised that he'd have regrets. "You wouldn't?"

"No. I told you I'd protect your reputation, and that's what I meant. I didn't think anybody we knew would be on that street. That was a mistake in judgment on my part. But, for the record, I don't think even a kiss would tell anyone that we're sleeping together."

"Well, from now on, we're not."

He looked upset. "We could still make this work."

"Maybe you could, but I couldn't." She felt very uncool, very boring, but she couldn't help it. "If my parents hadn't seen us kissing, then it might have been okay. But I know my mother, and after this little incident, she's going to be watching us very carefully for the rest of the weekend."

"I'll agree with you there, but don't you think the wedding will keep her distracted?"

"Not my mother. She's like one of those surveillance cameras in Circle K, constantly monitoring every aisle. I'd feel like I was back in high school trying to sneak out after curfew. No, thanks."

"But late at night, after everyone's asleep, we could—"

"I'm not taking that chance. I need to get my suitcase out of your suite, and I need to get it out before anybody knows it's there. I should have thought of that before we left."

They'd reached the lacquered front door of Townsend House. She took off her sunglasses and stuffed them in her purse. As she reached for the brass door handle, he grasped her arm gently.

She turned. "What?"

"This is how we'll do it. Don't come to the cottage. Let me pack up your stuff and take it to the reception desk. They must have someone who could bring it up to your room. That'll look a lot less suspicious."

"You're right. Thanks. That's very thoughtful." She suddenly realized that if she decided to stay away from him this weekend, this could be the last private conversation they'd have. It was a kind of goodbye— goodbye to twenty-four hours of unbelievable sexual excitement, goodbye to her first risk-taking opportunity. "Hugh, if we were dealing with any other circumstances, then..."

"But we aren't, and I'm not going to force the issue." He smiled. "Of course, if you change your mind, you know where I'll be. Oh, and while we're on that subject, I'm planning to pay for the cottage."

"No. That's my treat. It's the least I can do, considering everything."

He laughed and rubbed her arm with easy affection. "Considering everything, I should pay for the cottage and then some. Ever since we left the airport, I've had an amazing time with you. So I will certainly pay for the cottage. I'll stop by the reception desk before we leave for the rehearsal and take care of it."

"Darn it, I wish you wouldn't be so *nice*."

He sobered. "Yeah, I wish the same thing about you. I—"

The door opened, and Stuart came out. "Hey, guys!

Hugh, how's it going, buddy?" He grinned and shook Hugh's hand.

"I'm good," Hugh said. "Real good. You got those bridegroom jitters under control?"

Kate hadn't realized how tall Hugh was until he stood talking to Stuart, who was a couple of inches shorter.

"Just about." Stuart looked a little stressed as he combed his fingers through his brown hair. "That trip to Block Island was essential, though. Kim and I thought about staying out there and saying our vows on closed-circuit TV. You guys could set up a monitor in Belcourt Castle."

Kate laughed. "And after that I assume you'd both leave the country, because you could never come home again after a stunt like that."

"You understand what I'm saying, don't you, Hugh?" the groom asked.

"Most definitely."

Stuart looked from one to the other of them. "Let me give you both some advice. If you ever decide to do the deed, elope."

"You mean if either of us ever decides to do the deed," Kate said quickly. For a second there Stuart seemed to be making them into a couple.

"Right." Stuart glanced at them with a sparkle in his brown eyes. "That's what I meant. Listen, Hugh, Harry's upstairs getting dressed for the rehearsal. He's in Room Twelve. He said it'd been nearly a year since you two hooked up."

"That's right. I'll stop there before I go shower."

"Yeah, that reminds me. I'd better get moving. The bride asked me to run out and buy her a bottle of aspirin."

Kate frowned. "She has a headache?"

"Not yet. But with a full twenty-four hours left for more disaster to strike, my mom and stepmom are furious because they bought the same color of dress, and Gillian almost broke her ankle falling out of a tree this morning."

"Gillian is four," Kate explained to Hugh. "She's the niece of a bridesmaid, and she'll make a darling flower girl if they can get her into the outfit. She's a bit of a tomboy."

"Make that a *major* tomboy," Stuart said. "She sprained her ankle and skinned her nose, but it hasn't slowed her down one damned bit. Kim swears she's a lot like you."

Pretending to be brave but a big fat coward underneath? Yet Kate kept up the cheerful banter. Now was not the time for embarrassing self-revelation. "That makes her one terrific kid."

"Foolhardy was the word Kim used." Then he winked. "But I think that's a gross exaggeration. See you two at the rehearsal." He headed off down the walk.

Kate thought about her recent behavior and decided that *foolhardy* pretty well summed it up. This weekend was turning out to be a humbling experience.

Hugh glanced down at her. "So you used to climb trees as a kid?"

"I still do." It seemed like such a tame activity compared to jumping into bed with Hugh Armstrong, Hollywood stuntman. "You can get some awesome shots from up there."

"I'll bet."

Something about his tone made her peer at him more closely. "Are you okay?"

His smile flashed, cocky and assured. "Sure am. C'mon. Let's get this suitcase drop under control, so I can go see my brother. We both have a wedding rehearsal coming up and I *know* you don't want to be late."

SOON AFTERWARD, HUGH stood in the bedroom of the cottage and forced himself to pack Kate's suitcase quickly. It would be far too easy to linger over the scent of her perfume and the feel of her silky underwear. The room was full of her presence, and he was becoming more depressed by the minute.

He'd hung a Do Not Disturb sign on the door before leaving for the harbor, so the scene of the crime hadn't been disturbed. The outfit Kate had worn yesterday lay in a heap near the bed, right where she'd dropped it when she'd stripped for him. The condom box was still on her bedside table, too.

He tossed it in her suitcase. They were hers, after all. She had all the control, so she might as well have the condoms, too.

Right now was the moment when he was supposed to focus on her flaws so that he wouldn't be in such agony over her decision to end everything. Instead he was picturing her at four, a carrot-topped ball of energy who found the tallest tree in the neighborhood and climbed that sucker. If she was foolhardy, so was he.

Ah, but she wasn't quite as foolhardy as he was. She was smart enough to call a halt to this affair before it got out of hand. He should be thankful rather than miserable. The very fact that he was miserable should tell him he was in a precarious situation.

He zipped up the suitcase and left the cottage. Maybe meeting her parents had messed with his head. Now he saw Kate as part of a family, and he...hell, he wanted to be accepted by that family. Not likely, considering his intentions toward their daughter, so he needed to give up any fantasy of being chummy with the Coopers.

He found the same woman at the reception desk who'd checked him in the day before. "I was storing this temporarily for Ms. Kate Cooper." He hoisted Kate's black overnight bag. "Now it needs to be delivered to her room."

"I'll see to it." The woman regarded him with interest. "So we had you mixed up with your brother yesterday, didn't we?"

"Yeah. People say we could be twins."

She chuckled. "You know, I've always thought it would be fun to be a twin, especially if you looked exactly alike. Now Kate and Kim do, but with Kim wearing her hair in that Meg Ryan layered cut and Kate's so much shorter, I have no trouble telling them apart. You and Harry are harder, because you *really* look alike. I suppose people tell you that all the time."

He winked at her. "Never."

"I'll bet I could tell you apart now, though."

"Uh-huh. Harry's the one with the stethoscope permanently attached to his ears."

"Exactly." She smiled at him. "And you're the one with all the muscles."

Whoops. This was turning into a flirtation, and he didn't have the time—or the inclination, surprisingly. "All brawn and no brain," he said. "Listen, I happen to be on my way to Harry's room, so if Kate's is any-where nearby, I'll be glad to run this suitcase up for you."

"Oh. Well, certainly, if you like. She's in Room Eighteen, which connects with her sister's room. I guess the bridesmaids are planning a slumber party up there. I think it's so sweet that the bride and groom are staying in separate rooms tonight."

"Yeah." Hugh hadn't known that. His remaining hope that Kate might change her mind and slip away to the cottage dimmed. "By the way, I'll be picking up the tab for the cottage."

"That's not what I was told."

"I know. But that's the way I want it." He took out his wallet and handed her his credit card. "If you'll take care of that while I'm up talking to Harry, I'll be back by in a few minutes."

"Certainly, Mr. Armstrong." She looked as if she wanted to flirt some more.

Hugh kept his tone businesslike. "Thanks." He left the sitting room quickly and headed for the stairs, certain that he'd confused the hell out of the woman. Flirting had become a reflex and he'd always enjoyed the response until now. That was another bad sign that he was headed for a fall.

Upstairs he passed Number Twelve and continued on to Number Eighteen. He heard several women talking inside. Well, damn it. He'd brought the suitcase on the off chance that she'd be alone. She might never be alone again the entire weekend.

He had to rap hard before the conversation stopped and footsteps approached the door. It opened and he looked into green eyes that were almost Kate's eyes, but not quite. The mischief was missing.

The woman's eyes widened. "My God, you really do look exactly like Harry."

"You must be Kim." He glanced past her and saw that the room was a jumble of clothes and suitcases. There were three other women in the room, but he barely noticed what they looked like as his hungry gaze sought out Kate.

Wrapped in a bathrobe, she'd obviously just stepped out of the shower. She eyed him warily, and he knew she must be wondering why he'd brought the suitcase instead of having some member of the staff deliver it.

"Hi, Kate," he said. "Somebody downstairs said you needed this, and I was on my way up to see Harry, so I offered to bring it to you."

"Thanks." The hair at her neckline was damp, exactly as it had been when he'd found her in the whirlpool that morning.

"You're welcome." As he stood there thinking about what had happened in the whirlpool, he almost missed the fact that Kim had spoken to him. He glanced down at her. "I'm sorry. What did you say?"

"I asked if you enjoyed your sail this afternoon." She gazed at him with a curious smile.

"Yes." And he didn't dare spend any time remembering what he and Kate had done in that sailboat or he was liable to embarrass everyone, including himself. Kim apparently suspected something was going on, and all she had to do was talk to her parents to have it confirmed. "Hey, I know you all have to get ready, so I'll take off. Kate, I'll meet you downstairs in about twenty minutes."

She nodded.

This was all wrong, he thought. She should be with

him, down in that cottage, not up here pretending she didn't care about him. He had the insane urge to march in there and throw her over his shoulder. Something was going seriously haywire in his brain for him to be having thoughts like that.

She was just another woman. In two more days she'd be a memory.

But he didn't believe a word of it as he turned away from her door. He had a strong feeling that sometime in the past few hours his life had changed, and it was never changing back.

As he walked toward Harry's room he had the distinct impression that Kim was watching him and that she knew exactly how deep he'd fallen. As they said in the cop movies, he'd been made.

11

THE MINUTE KIM CLOSED the door, Kate raced across the room to grab her overnight case so she could escape into the bathroom again.

Kim was quicker. She pulled it out of reach. "Not until you 'fess up, girl!"

"Yeah, is he a hottie, or what? Just like his brother!" Ruth bounced on the bed like a six-year-old. Her dark curly hair bounced with her.

"I wanna know if you're hooked up with him or not." Sabrina's blue eyes shone with eagerness. Long, lithe and blond, she sat with her legs tucked under her in the lotus position. "Because you acted *très* disinterested. So if you don't want him, I think I just met my karma for the weekend."

"I can't believe we have a matched set of these guys." Bette, a highlighted brunette, lounged on the bed and munched a candy bar. "If Kate's got a lock on this one, maybe I can check out the other one, what's-his-name. Dr. Harry."

"Hang on, *I've* got dibs on Dr. Harry," Ruth said.

"Do not!" Bette said. "Damn, but I shoulda lost those ten pounds before this weekend. Maybe I should starve myself between now and the wedding, go on a twenty-four-hour fast." She frowned. "But then I might faint."

Kim put the suitcase behind her and crossed her

arms. "No point in suffering until we know the situation. Kate, you were weird on the phone this morning, and just now the guy's tongue was dragging the floor, but you pretended he was, like, no more important than the bellman. What's up?"

Kate gazed at her sister, who knew her inside and out. Then she glanced around at their three best friends. They'd bonded with Ruth and Sabrina in first grade. Bette had moved to Providence in fifth and the gang had immediately appropriated her because she made them all laugh until they peed their pants. If Kate had imagined she could keep a secret from any of these women, she'd been delusional.

So she told them the whole story—or most of the story. She toned down the sex, because even best friends didn't need to know those kinds of details. She also made it very clear that Hugh was interested in a weekend fling, not a long-term relationship, and that until her parents had caught them kissing in public, she'd been ready to go along with his plan.

By the time she finished talking, they were all staring at her with their mouths open, and Stuart was pounding on the door.

"Hey, we're late!" he yelled. "Get a move on, ladies!"

"You can't tell *anybody*," Kate said.

They all looked insulted.

"I mean you *really* can't tell," Kate added as she reached for her suitcase and quickly unzipped it while Stuart continued to bang on the door.

"We won't," Kim promised quietly. Then she raised her voice. "All right, Stuart! Don't break it down! We're almost ready!"

"If we're not at the Belcourt in ten minutes they'll cancel the rehearsal!" Stuart sounded very agitated.

"I'm so sorry." Kate started pulling things out of her suitcase, looking for the outfit she'd planned to wear that night. "I'm making everyone late, as usual, and I—" She stopped abruptly as she jerked out a pair of capris and the condom box sailed out with them, spilling its contents on the floor.

"Too perfect!" Bette slid off the bed and started grabbing condoms. "Just what this weekend needed."

And they all plopped to the floor, snatching up condoms and laughing as they pelted each other with them.

All except Kate. "Stop, stop!" She wasn't used to being the responsible party, but everyone seemed to have forgotten about the rehearsal. "Hey, we have to get going!"

Kim staggered to her feet, still laughing. "Attention, everybody." She cleared her throat. "The bride has an announcement to make. We are canceling the rehearsal."

"No!" Kate threw off the bathrobe she'd borrowed and pawed around for her underwear. "I can make it! You guys go ahead, and I'll drive over. I'll be right behind you. I can—"

"Nope." Kim put her hands on her hips. "This is exactly the kind of thing Stuart and I talked about during our little retreat on Block Island. We promised ourselves that we'd bend the schedule to fit the people, not vice versa. Come to think of it, I like the idea of going with no rehearsal. That will make the ceremony more spontaneous and less formal."

"Well said," Bette agreed. "We don't need no stinkin' rehearsal. Hell, the five of us have been to a gazillion weddings. If we can't muddle through this, we're truly pathetic."

Kate found her underwear and put it on. "Well, I feel like it's all my fault."

"Forget about it," Kim said. "This is for the best."

"What about Gillian, though?" Ruth asked. "I think Andrea wanted her to do at least one walk-through. She's never been a flower girl before."

"She'll be fine," Kim said. "Even if she screws up, it'll be comic relief. No problem." Then she walked over to the door and opened it a crack. "Stuart?"

"Yeah? What's going on in there? Sounds like a circus. Are you—"

"We're going to bag the rehearsal."

"Why?"

"Because."

On the other side of the door, there was a long pause.

Kate looked at her friends and stifled a giggle.

"That's it?" Stuart said, clearly baffled. "Just *because?*"

"That's it," Kim said. "So if you'll kindly call the Belcourt and notify them and Reverend Applegate, that would be great."

"But—"

"We can go over our vows during Happy Hour at the restaurant. Oh, and please call Andrea and tell her the rehearsal's canceled, but we're sure Gillian will be fine."

After another long pause, Stuart uttered a resigned, "Okay." Then he left.

Kim closed the door, and Bette sighed dramatically. "Oh, Kim, he's going to make a *wonderful* husband. He didn't argue or anything."

"That's because he doesn't really want to go to the rehearsal either." Kim glanced at Kate. "And now that we have a little spare time, let's figure out how we can cover for you."

"Cover? What do you mean?"

"C'mon, Kate. If we can take Mom and Dad out of the equation, wouldn't you like to have your weekend fling, after all?"

AS HUGH SAT SEPARATED from Kate by miles of restaurant table crowded with plates, food and glasses, he tried to figure out what had happened after he'd left her suitcase in the roomful of women. Something had gone down in that room, something that had caused the rehearsal to be canceled. But Kim and her bridesmaids seemed to have closed ranks to keep him away from Kate, and Kate was the only one he felt comfortable asking about the whole strange development.

Eliminating the rehearsal meant that nobody had to drive because the restaurant was within walking distance of the Townsend House. Once Kate, Kim and the bridesmaids had finally trooped downstairs, the whole wedding party had formed a noisy brigade that marched to the harborside restaurant Kim and Stuart had picked for the rehearsal dinner.

During that procession and all during the dinner that followed, Hugh couldn't shake the feeling that the bridesmaids knew what had happened between him and Kate. They seemed to pay no attention to him whatsoever, other than being normally polite, but every once in a while he'd catch one of them giving him a look. Yeah, they knew. Kate had told them.

That sort of irritated him, after the way she'd carried on about not mentioning it to a soul. But it was her secret to tell or not tell, so he'd keep his end of the bargain. Harry suspected something was up, though. When Hugh had stopped by Harry's room after dropping off the suitcase, Harry had seen right through his nonchalance and had point-blank asked what was wrong. Hugh had shrugged off the question and made a quick exit with the excuse that he had to shower.

Since then Harry and Hugh hadn't been alone. The party was becoming loud and boisterous, as all good rehearsal dinners should be, Hugh thought, especially when the participants had totally skipped the rehearsal. While they'd all waited for their food to arrive, Reverend Applegate had created a little diorama of the wedding setup on the long table by using glassware, silverware and the salt and pepper shakers.

Kim had been a stemmed goblet and Stuart a sturdy water glass. Kate was the pepper, which Hugh thought was appropriate, and Harry was the salt. The bridesmaids were forks, the groomsmen spoons, and when the parents of the bride and groom refused to be knives, the minister had substituted drink coasters. Gillian, the little flower girl, was represented by a sugar packet. From what Hugh could gather, her mother had decided to keep her home and get her to bed early instead of bringing her to the restaurant.

Hugh sat between Stuart's stepmother, the vegetarian, and Nick, Kate's rolling-stone brother. Nick had inherited his mother's coloring and didn't look a lot like Kate, but every once in a while Hugh saw a reflection of her in the curve of Nick's mouth or the lift of an eyebrow. He liked Nick, but he was sure John and Emily Cooper had told Nick about the kiss-on-the-street incident, because Kate's brother treated him with caution.

Harry was directly across the table. Stuart had badgered them into doing their identical twin thing— a pantomime in which Hugh mirrored Harry's every movement. They'd been performing the pantomime since they were ten, but Hugh nearly screwed up the ancient routine because he was so distracted by Kate down at the far end of the long table. Their corny slapstick was a hit, anyway. With all the liquor being consumed, Hugh thought a fifth-rate flea circus would be a hit.

Moments later Harry announced that the waitress was taking entirely too long bringing another round of Long Island Iced Teas. "Come on, bro. Let's go see if we can find those drinks ourselves," he said.

Hugh was sure Harry was creating an opportunity to grill him, but he couldn't very well refuse to help the best man keep the guests well oiled. "Be glad to," he said.

Sure enough, the minute they were out of earshot of the table, Harry started in. "You haven't taken your eyes off Kate Cooper all night. Are you going to tell me what's going on?"

"Should I?" Hugh aimed for the bar. He'd been taking it easy on the booze, so he thought he could outwit Harry, who was rediscovering his fondness for Long Island Iced Tea.

"Let me put it this way," Harry said. "You look like you need a friend, and I'm your best bet."

Hugh sighed. "I'll be okay."

"Not from where I'm sitting. Or walking." Harry chuckled. "Or weaving, actually. Whatever. I've seen you with a lot of girls, and this is a whole new you. The brother I know has never drooled openly."

"I'm not drooling."

"The hell you're not." They'd reached the bar. "Just a sec. Let me get this handled." He conferred with the bartender and found out the drink order had been misplaced, so he put in a new one and said they'd take it back to the table themselves.

Then he turned his back to the bar and leaned against it. "Okay, I know you spent all day with her. Stuart told me. Now you're acting strange, and so's she, for that matter. And another thing, her folks are giving both of you the hairy eyeball."

Hugh wondered if his brother was soused enough to forget all of this after tonight. It would be a relief to unburden himself to someone, and Harry was right—he couldn't do any better than his twin brother.

He decided to explain as much as he could without revealing anything he'd promised to keep secret. "You know how I always look for a fatal flaw, so I won't get hung up on anybody?"

"Oh, yeah. The fatal flaw concept. Did I ever tell you I thought that was bullshit?"

Hugh shoved his hands in his pockets and stared at the neon Budweiser sign hanging over the back of the bar. "Yep. And I guess it is, because this time it isn't working."

"Holy moly. You've found the perfect woman."

"Isn't that a kick in the head?" Hugh met his brother's gaze. "I can't find a damn thing wrong with her. She's getting to me, bro."

"I never thought I'd see the day. But I notice the two of you are not, like, together."

"You noticed that, huh? Well, part of that's my

fault, because I'm scared to death, and the other part is, she's looking for a genuine hero, not some slob who pretends to be a hero for the benefit of the camera."

Harry blew out a breath. "There's your fatal flaw. She's an idiot."

"No, she's not! She's right! I don't pretend to be a prize. I can't imagine any woman would want to hook up with me for the long haul. I'm not—"

"Damn it, Hugh, when are you gonna stop running?"

Hugh stared at him. They'd never really talked about this, and undoubtedly Harry wouldn't have brought it up now, except that he was mildly sloshed. "When are you?" Hugh countered. "You've dated enough nurses to staff a hospital, but this is the closest to the altar you've ever come, being best man for Stuart."

"Yeah, I know." Harry gave him a lopsided grin. "There's a shrink at the hospital who has me all figured out."

"And?"

The grin slipped a little. "She told me the only way I'll ever get over that thing with Joe is if I make a commitment to somebody, take a risk."

Hugh rubbed the back of his neck. "I take risks all the time, and I'm not over it."

"She meant *emotional* risks, buddy-boy. She said I'm stuck in the phase where I think it's too chancy to care about somebody."

"You care about your patients, and don't tell me you don't."

"I never let them get that close. Not like I did with big brother Joe."

Hugh knew exactly what Harry was talking about.

You could be kind and compassionate without ever letting people in where you lived. Kate was the first person he'd ever felt like dropping his guard for. "You still have nightmares?"

"Yeah. You?"

"Yeah. Not so much anymore." Hugh noticed their drinks were sitting on a tray and the bartender was starting their way. "The drinks are ready, and we need to get back. You have duties."

Harry pushed away from the bar. "Look, if Kate is wonderful, and she'd have to be the way you're acting, then I think...I think you'd better give it a shot."

"Easy for you to say. What's that line—*physician, heal thyself*?"

"I'm working on it," Harry said. "When I meet the right woman, somebody who affects me like Kate's affecting you, I'll work harder."

"But Kate wants a hero."

"So be a hero. Sweep her off her feet." Harry gave him an off-center, cocky smile, as if to signal that the serious stuff was over for now. "You're just nervous because you've never had to try that before."

KATE HAD AGREED TO THE plan cooked up by her friends, which meant that in public she had to stay far away from Hugh and act as if she'd lost all interest in him. Kim didn't think that would completely fool their parents, but it would prevent the rumors from spreading. The plan made sense to Kate, but the execution of it was killing her.

The rehearsal dinner from hell seemed to go on forever. Her only salvation was to take a bunch of pictures and focus on Kim and Stuart's happiness. Even watching them had a sharp edge to it, though. Kim had found the man of her dreams, while the best Kate could do was spend a few wild and lust-filled hours in the arms of a man who would leave on Sunday, never to be seen again.

In the twenty-six years Kate had been Kim's twin, the two of them had traded places dozens of times, but it had been a temporary game. Kate had never actually wanted to be in Kim's shoes, but tonight she did. She envied the twin who was about to marry the right guy, a guy whose interest extended beyond a weekend of sex.

Eventually the evening broke up, with the group dividing into three parts. The parents headed home to bed, the groom and his buddies went bar-hopping, while Kim, Kate and their friends gathered in their suite of rooms for an old-fashioned slumber party. The women planned to tell no one that sometime during the night Kate would sneak down to Hugh's cottage.

"I figured out how we'll know when the guys come home and Hugh will be back in his lair," Kim said as they all changed into pajamas and pulled out the manicure supplies. "I made Stuart promise to page me before he goes to bed, so we can tell each other goodnight."

"You realize that could be four in the morning," Bette said. "Which gives Kate almost zero time with her hunk of burning love. Plus her sugar baby could be stewed to the gills."

"It won't be four in the morning," Kim said. "Stuart's tired, and Harry's been working those long hours at the hospital, so neither of them will be up to staying out late. I can't promise what Hugh's condition will be when Kate gets down there, but I predict I'll hear from

Stuart before my second coat of polish is dry. Now, who wants the honor of giving the bride a manicure?"

For the next two hours Kate tried to throw herself into the festivities as they lounged on the two double beds giving each other manicures and pedicures while reminiscing about the pranks they'd pulled in high school. She partly succeeded, but too many times she'd glance at the clock and her stomach would start to churn.

Finally she couldn't stand the suspense. "You know what? I've decided not to go down there after all," she announced. "This is crazy, to get all involved with some guy who's leaving on Sunday."

"Then maybe I'll go," Bette said with a wink. "In the dark and with a few drinks in him, he might not know the difference."

Kate was instantly consumed with jealousy. "I don't—"

"Just kidding!" Bette said. "But you should have seen your face. You were ready to kill me."

"Go down there." Sabrina took the cotton from between her toes and looked over at Kate. "You never know how this will turn out."

"Yes, I do. He told me straight out. And that's why I'm going to stay here." As she was congratulating herself on making the right, though cowardly, decision, Kim's pager went off.

Kim scooped it up from the nightstand and looked at the number. "That's Stuart's room phone. They're back." She gazed at Kate.

Kate's shrug was designed to cover up the fact that she was quivering. "Yeah, well, I'm not going down there."

Bette started making clucking noises, and soon Sabrina and Ruth joined in.

"I'm not chicken, damn it!" Kate was lying through her teeth and she knew it. "I just don't see the point!"

Kim gave her a nudge. "The point is that you've been bitching and moaning about your boring life. This is your chance to spice it up, and if you don't go down there, I don't want to hear another word about how nothing exciting ever happens to you."

Kate met her sister's relentlessly honest stare. Kim had the annoying habit of being right. It was so much easier to complain than take action. If she spent the rest of the night with Hugh she'd probably end up with a broken heart, but so what? At least she'd be grabbing life by the lapels, instead of standing a safe distance away while claiming she craved drama.

It was put up or shut up time. She swung her legs to the floor and stood. Anticipation and fear battled it out in her stomach, much the way they did when she was about to step into the first car of a giant roller coaster ride. "I'll go, but if he's drunk, I'm coming straight back here."

"See, we should've found a way to tip him off about this," Ruth said. "Pass him a note like I said, so he'd go easy on the booze."

Kim shook her head. "Too risky. Notes get intercepted."

"Kim's right," Kate said. "This was the only way." She walked over to her suitcase in the corner of the room, and her hands trembled as she took off her pajamas and pulled on the capris and knit top she'd worn to the rehearsal dinner.

"Now remember what you're going to tell someone if you get caught in the halls," Sabrina said.

Kate nodded. "I need to get my dress from storage and check the hem length with my new shoes."

"Very good," Ruth said. "Have we thought of everything?"

"God, no." Bette snatched up a couple of condoms from the nightstand where they'd tossed them earlier. "Don't forget some of these. How many do you need?"

"Take the whole box," Ruth said, laughing.

"That would be inconspicuous, all right." Kim screwed the top on her nail polish. "Wandering the halls of the Townsend House with a box of condoms."

"Will you all cut it out?" Even though these were her best friends, she couldn't help blushing. But she needed the condoms. "I'll take two."

"Take three." Bette held them out. "The guy strikes me as a real stud."

Kate rolled her eyes as she took the condoms. She had no pockets in her capris, so she tucked them inside the waistband. "This is like those *Fractured Fairy Tales* we used to watch on TV. Cinderella and her fairy godmothers passing out condoms."

"Fairy godmothers of the new millennium always remember birth control," Bette said. "Now get going, already!"

"I'm going!" Kate left the room before she lost her nerve.

ONCE KATE WAS GONE, the other women remained silent for several seconds while they stared at the door.

Finally, when it didn't open again, Bette spoke. "Okay, Kim, do you think he's going home on Sunday like he says?"

Kim blew out a breath. "God, I hope not. He'd be such a fool."

"He watched her all night long." Ruth wrapped her arms around her knees. "I think he's crazy about her."

"So do I," said Sabrina. "And she may think that a stuntman isn't who she wants, but she wants him. She wants him bad."

Kim looked at her bridesmaids. "That's why I pushed her to go down there, because I have a feeling that this could be it for both of them, but if I'm wrong..."

"I don't think you're wrong," Bette said.

"You'd better hope I'm not." Kim massaged her scalp to loosen the tension collecting there. "Because if I am wrong and he leaves on Sunday, I'll be on my honeymoon and you guys will have to pick up the pieces."

12

HUGH ROAMED THROUGH the cottage, unable to settle down. After he flipped on the television, he turned it off. Then he fooled around looking for a decent FM station, and once he found one, listened for about ten seconds before shutting that off, too. Finally he brushed his teeth, but instead of going to bed, he wandered around some more.

Sack time would be a very good idea. He'd had damned little sleep for the past two nights. But he dreaded climbing into the bed he'd shared with Kate, and he was really irritated with himself about that. Exhibiting behavior totally unlike him, he'd become sentimental about her. Everything in the cottage tugged at him, depressing him with memories of the great time they'd had together and reminding him that those great times were over.

Harry had advised him to sweep Kate off her feet. Harry had also been too schnockered to realize that wouldn't be possible. Kate might as well be in a convent up in that suite with her girlfriends. As for tomorrow, from the way Stuart had described the wedding day schedule, the men and women would continue to be separated until the ceremony. That left tomorrow night for Hugh to dazzle Kate and show her that he could be a hero.

Even if he could accomplish that kind of miracle, he

wasn't convinced it was a good idea. Harry was letting this shrink convince him to change, but that didn't mean such a thing was possible. Hugh didn't want Kate to become some kind of guinea pig in an experiment to see if he was capable of a real relationship.

He continued to cruise around the cottage while trying to work up some enthusiasm for going to bed. The maid had been here while he was at the rehearsal dinner. She'd changed the bed, turned down the sheets and placed fresh roses in the vases. The scent of the roses seemed to mock him.

At last he identified the emotion he was feeling, and he wasn't any happier once he had. For the first time in years, he was lonely.

With a sigh he unbuttoned his shirt, took it off and tossed it on a chair in the bedroom. Then he sat on the chair and pulled off his shoes and socks. He had to try and get some sleep, and he'd have no chance of that prowling around the cottage. Maybe once he stretched out on the bed, exhaustion would take over.

He was so deep in thought that he didn't register the sound of a light tapping until after it stopped. Pausing in the act of unbuckling his belt, he listened closely. His mind could be playing tricks on him, or a branch might have brushed the window.

Or Kate was out there. He hurried to the front door and opened it. Fog had rolled in, softening the outline of the rosebushes and creating haloes around the low security lights. He could just make out Kate in the haze, already halfway back to the main house. The special effects wizards in Hollywood couldn't have done a better job of making Kate look ethereal and out of reach, maybe even a figment of his imagination.

But he was a realist, so he knew this wasn't some

sort of paranormal event taking place in the rose garden. She was really there, walking quietly back to the main house so her footsteps couldn't be heard by anyone. She'd snuck out to be with him and had decided he was asleep.

He should let her go, let this thing die between them. The thought swirled through his brain and was gone, because he couldn't let her go, not when she'd made the effort to come to him in spite of all the reasons not to. Her appearance gave a huge boost to his sagging ego.

Heart pounding, he started after her, wincing as his bare feet touched the damp chill of the flagstone walkway. "Kate," he said in a low voice.

She spun around, her eyes wide in the soft glow from the fog-shrouded lights. Dampness glistened in her hair and on her skin as she stood there breathing rapidly, her lips parted in surprise. "I...I thought you were asleep."

"No." No matter how much of a realist he was, he still had trouble believing that she was here, considering how worried she'd been that someone would find out about them. Maybe he really had fallen asleep and was dreaming this. But he didn't think you could smell things in a dream, and he was very aware of the scent of roses mixed with the tangy salt air and the loamy essence of freshly turned dirt.

Her gaze moved over his bare chest, his unbuckled belt and his bare feet. "But you're...tired. You were going to bed."

"I was going to bed, but I'm not tired." A hero wouldn't stand there staring at the woman of his dreams. A hero would act. He closed the distance between them and gathered her into his arms.

She felt so damn good, so damn perfect there. Once he touched her warmth and his body absorbed the slight trembling of hers, once he caught the aroma of her special perfume, the right words came. "I was waiting for you." Then he scooped her up and carried her back to the cottage.

KATE HADN'T BEEN CARRIED since she was a little girl. This was so not like that. Hugh held her close to his bare chest and she could feel the rapid thumping of his heart, the heat of his skin. The musky scent of aroused male mingled with the sweet smell of roses as he gazed into her eyes and shouldered his way through the door.

He kicked it closed with the side of his foot, like a karate master. He was easily the most virile man she'd ever known. Faux hero or not, he could turn her on in a matter of seconds. With Hugh, being carried to bed was a potent form of foreplay. She was getting hotter with every step he took.

He didn't bother to ask her why she'd come to the cottage or even why she'd changed her mind. He must not care how she'd escaped unnoticed or if she planned to keep this rendezvous a secret. Apparently it was enough that she was there, and his immediate reaction went beyond all her expectations.

He truly lived for the moment, and so would she. This was, after all, what she'd longed for—an intense passion that silenced all questions, eliminated all roadblocks. A need so great that it had to be acted on *now*, and nothing else in the world mattered.

After laying her on the bed, he slipped off her mules and tossed them to the floor. He left the light on as he began undressing her, marking his progress with hot kisses. She wiggled happily out of her clothes, eager to expose more skin and collect more kisses.

Gradually the nervous tremors eased and she grew languid with desire. There was something to be said for experience. Quite a bit to be said for experience. Oh, yes. There. And there. Her body began to sing along with the seductive tune he played with his mouth and tongue. What a fool she'd been to think of denying herself this incredible pleasure.

When he found the three condoms tucked inside the waistband of her capris, he glanced into her eyes. "Planning to stay a while?" he murmured.

She hoped the number didn't look like some demand on her part. "We don't have to use them all." Her voice had dropped a register and sounded as if she'd swallowed some of the fog blanketing the harbor. She loved this new, sexy voice.

"Oh, we can use them all." He laid them on the nightstand and continued his erotic task of revealing her. "I hope you put a few in your panties, too." He tugged the elastic down.

She lifted her hips, more than happy to cooperate. "I didn't bring any more."

"Too bad." He trailed kisses along the insides of her thighs as he stripped off her panties.

She could barely breathe, she was so excited.

"I guess we'll make do with what we have." His breath tickled the damp skin of her inner thigh. Then he proceeded to make do very nicely.

She writhed against the soft sheets as he showed her once again that he had a talented tongue and wasn't afraid to use it. Teasing and coaxing her until she was gasping, he finally gave her a shattering climax that left her delirious. She barely noticed that he'd shed his own clothes and opened one of the condom packets until he moved over her and leaned down to nibble at her lips.

"All through dinner I thought about loving you like this." He eased the tip of his penis inside, caressing her gently.

She wrapped her arms around him, kneading the powerful muscles of his back as she looked up into his eyes. "It was a long dinner."

"A very long dinner." He slid in a little more. "Especially when you'd made it clear that I couldn't make love to you again tonight."

Smoothing her hands down his back, she pressed her fingertips into his firm bottom. "Dumb decision." Then she lifted her hips and urged him closer.

With a groan, he buried himself deep. "Maybe not so dumb," he said, his voice tight with leashed passion, his blue eyes dark with mounting desire. "But I'm very glad you changed your mind."

She drank in his intensity. She might be only a temporary diversion, but that wasn't how he was looking at her. For tonight she'd pretend that all her fantasies were true and he was the man she was meant to find. Tonight they would make love in a fog-shrouded cottage surrounded by roses.

"I'm right where I need to be," she said.

"So am I." He began stroking her slowly and deliberately. "So am I."

Holding his gaze, she caught his rhythm as they moved like dancers responding to an ever faster beat. The perfection and beauty of it was her reward for daring to take a chance tonight. How unthinkable that she'd find such pleasure and then have it taken away. But that was the danger she'd accepted in exchange for ecstasy. With that thought, she abandoned herself to the wonder of how effortlessly his body undulated against hers.

Together they climbed and together they fell, clutching each other and crying out with joy. As the storm of sensation receded, Kate knew that if this was all she would ever have, it would have to be enough.

THEY SHOWERED TO KEEP themselves awake and played in the spray until they had to make use of a second condom. Then exhaustion claimed them, and they decided to turn off the lights for a short nap. They promised themselves they wouldn't sleep long, and Hugh guaranteed that by setting the alarm clock, although Kate tried to talk him out of it. She was beginning to feel guilty about all the sleep she'd stolen from him.

Minutes before the alarm would go off, Kate was jerked awake by Hugh flailing around and moaning in distress. Heart pounding, she scrambled to a sitting position. Then she realized he was having a nightmare.

She shook him gently, hoping that would be enough to ease him out of the bad dream. Even though they'd shared incredible sex, there were so many things she didn't know about him, and listening in on his nightmare seemed like an invasion of privacy. She was uncomfortable, and she could bet he'd be embarrassed by his vulnerability. Better for him to shift dreams without waking up.

But he was deep into the nightmare and didn't awaken. He called out a man's name, drawing out the single syllable of what sounded like Joe. "No, oh, nooooo!" he cried. Then he shuddered, and the strangled sound coming from his throat was half groan, half sob.

Kate couldn't bear to listen to him in such agony. So he'd be embarrassed. There were worse things—like terrible dreams that made him cry. Grabbing his shoulder, she shook him hard. "Hugh! Hugh, wake up!"

"What?" He bolted upright, wide awake. "What's wrong?"

How tender he seemed at that moment, how desperately in need of comfort. She'd thought of him as such a tough guy, but maybe she'd been wrong. "You had a bad dream," she said softly. Then she laid her hand against his cheek and discovered it was wet with tears. "A really bad dream."

"Oh." Instead of drawing her close and confiding in her, he pulled away and climbed out of bed. "Charming," he said in a voice filled with disgust. "Sorry about that."

His withdrawal hurt, but she could understand it. He was obviously very embarrassed. "Hugh, don't apologize." She tried to ease his discomfort. "Everybody has nightmares. It's no big—"

"Damn it," he muttered, cutting off her attempt to smooth things over by stalking toward the bathroom.

She felt very alone as she listened to him running water and splashing it on his face. Someone ought to put out a manual on how to conduct brief affairs, she thought forlornly. In an awkward situation like this, she wasn't sure whether to follow him or leave him alone. She wanted to know about the nightmare that had seized him so strongly, but as a temporary lover, she hesitated to ask.

Eventually he came back into the bedroom. His

heavy sigh wasn't promising. "Kate, I'm sorry, but this isn't working."

She reeled from the finality of that statement. Even though she'd braced herself for a parting of the ways, it wasn't supposed to happen like this. Sure, she'd called a halt before, but he'd taken it well and she'd known they could always pick up again at any time.

So she had picked it up, and he'd seemed very happy about that. Unconsciously she'd scripted a new ending to their story. After a weekend of mutual pleasure they would hug and have a last kiss. Then he'd walk away, and she'd stay behind, a brave smile on her face. Instead he seemed about to reject her before the weekend was over.

"Because of a nightmare?" She tried to make out his expression in the dim light.

"In a way." He cleared his throat. "I thought I could be your hero, at least for the weekend, but it seems I'm not up to that. Somebody mixed up the cue cards on me."

"I don't understand." Her insides felt like lead.

"Kate, you're not the type for a weekend affair, and certainly not a weekend affair with a guy like me."

"How can you say that after the way we..." She couldn't find the courage to finish the sentence with *make love* and she refused to finish it with *enjoy sex*. They'd had more than sex, and he damned well knew it. She'd seen it in his eyes.

"That's part of the problem," he said gently. "You've cut through my defenses and stirred things up, things I'm finally starting to get control of."

"Like nightmares?"

"Yes, that's part of it. The point is, I can't afford what you're liable to cost me. And you shouldn't be wasting yourself on a bum like me. I'm not a hero. I'm just a guy who does a good job of pretending to be one."

Her throat tightened as tears threatened. She'd once thought the same thing about him, but now...now she wasn't so sure about that. "What if I disagree with you?"

"It's a free country, so you can disagree all you want. But I'm not going to give you the chance to find out how right I am." He leaned down, picked up the clothes he'd left on the floor and began putting them on.

"What are you doing?"

"Getting dressed so I can take a walk out by the harbor. That'll give you space to...to..."

"Get the hell out of your cottage?" Anger came as a welcome relief from bitter disappointment.

"Kate, this is the best thing for both of us." He sat in the chair and shoved his bare feet into his loafers. "Believe me."

"Kindly speak for yourself and don't be so worried about protecting me. I don't think this is about me, after all. I think it's about you, and that yellow streak running down the middle of *your* back." Never mind that she'd been acting like a coward until Kim had pushed her into coming down here. She'd conquered her fears and decided to go for broke. She was furious with him for lacking the courage to do the same.

He grabbed his shirt and pulled it on, his movements jerky. "You're right. I'm a coward. You need to find a guy with the guts to love you." Then he left, buttoning his shirt on the way.

Love her? Who had been talking about love? Not her, that's for sure. She'd only wanted sexual excitement, and he was letting a nightmare put a stop to that. But *love?* Once she'd recovered from her mistake in thinking Hugh was the hero she'd been waiting for, she'd never given love another thought.

Except there was that one moment tonight, when he'd been deep inside her and she'd looked into his eyes. Something had passed between them then, something significant. Something powerful.

But it hadn't been love, she decided, climbing out of the bed and gathering her clothes. If he felt love for her, he wouldn't have walked out like this. And if she felt love for him, then she wouldn't have the urge to shake him until his teeth rattled.

She really didn't know what to think. But one thing she did know—tomorrow would be a very long day.

HUGH DIDN'T RETURN to the cottage until dawn, and all the walking he'd done allowed him only a couple of hours of sleep. When he woke up, his sense of survival told him that he'd better throw himself into this wedding or he'd be a basket case by Sunday. Making a call to Harry, he invited his brother, Stuart and the groomsmen to hang out at the cottage for the day.

They all seemed happy to do that once they'd stocked the refrigerator with beer, ordered pizza and turned on Sports Center. Hugh invited Kate's brother Nick, too, but he hoped Nick would turn him down. Fortunately Nick said that he and his dad were spending the day at Belcourt Castle checking out photo ops with the wedding photographer.

Hugh had a brief moment of pity for the poor guy Kim and Stuart had hired to shoot the wedding and reception. Working a wedding for a family of photographers had to be a nightmare. No matter what he did, they'd think of ways he could have done it better. Hugh wondered if Kate would be able to resist smuggling her little thirty-five millimeter into the wedding. He'd bet his Corvette she'd have it concealed on her somewhere.

Mostly Hugh tried not to think about Kate, which was why he'd surrounded himself with a bunch of noisy guys. His strategy worked for most of the day as he joked with Harry and Stuart and got to know the groomsmen. Before meeting Kate at the airport, this was exactly the kind of scene he'd imagined when he'd planned to attend the wedding, and he definitely was enjoying himself. Sure he was. Five whole minutes at a time would go by in which he didn't think about Kate.

Then Harry found the third, unused condom that Hugh had forgotten was still lying on the nightstand.

Hugh supposed he should have been grateful that Harry didn't announce his find to the entire group of guys. Instead he pocketed the condom and waited until Hugh went into the kitchen area to score another beer. Then Harry followed him.

When Hugh asked his brother if he wanted another beer, too, Harry took out the condom and tossed it on the counter. "Look what I found."

"Shit." Hugh grabbed it and stuffed it in his pocket as he glanced back into the living room. The guys remained glued to the tube. No one had seen anything. "I forgot about that."

Harry kept his voice low, and the baseball game on the wide-screen TV covered his comments. "Y'know, normally I would stay totally out this, but now that I'm getting to know the Coopers, I can't."

Hugh's fingers tightened around the cold beer can

as he gazed at his brother. "Sure, you can. There's nothing for you to worry about, bro."

"Isn't there? In your life, these little square packages don't travel solo. I'm guessing there used to be more, and this is the leftover one. So you spent last night playing horizontal hopscotch. Am I right?"

Hugh could kick himself for not remembering to put away the condom. Popping open the beer, he took a swallow to buy some time. He couldn't lie to Harry, not even if he wanted to. "I'll neither confirm nor deny," he said at last.

"Oh, don't give me that *West Wing* jargon. We both know what's going on and who it's going on with. Just tell me if you're planning to finish what you start, or if you're going to ride off into the sunset, like usual."

Technically, Harry was older—by a minute—and Hugh couldn't believe how that one minute seemed to make a difference in their personalities. "Sometimes you carry this older brother business too far."

"Or not far enough. I tried to tell you this last night. We both need to wake up before it's too late. Don't blow this. For your sake as much as hers."

Hugh lowered his voice even more. "I *am* thinking of her, damn it. That's why I sent her away this morning." It had been one of the hardest things he'd ever done, but he believed in the rightness of it.

Harry groaned and gently banged his head several times against the refrigerator door. "You're hopeless."

Hugh bristled. "I don't see you with a happily-ever-after girl on your arm, either, stud."

"I said I'm working on that. I'm looking. One thing I'm *not* doing is sending the perfect woman away when she shows up."

Hugh looked at the beer can in his hand and knew if

he gripped it any tighter he'd dent the aluminum. He relaxed his hold. "How many times do I have to say this? She doesn't want a stuntman from Hollywood."

"How do you know?" Harry sent him a challenging look. "Have you asked her?"

13

THE FRANTIC PACE OF THE wedding day was both a blessing and a curse for Kate—a blessing because she was too busy to think about Hugh and a curse because she wanted to crawl away by herself and lick her wounds. That wouldn't be possible until the weekend was over.

She'd discovered her sister and friends were asleep by the time she'd returned to the room in the early morning. She'd spent hours staring into the darkness, while the others had overslept. It was fortunate for her because that made the schedule so tight no one had time to quiz Kate about her adventure with Hugh.

The bridal party was barely awake by the time Kim's favorite hairdresser arrived at the Townsend House to create hairstyles for everyone. The challenge turned out to be Kate, because the flowered headpieces required a certain amount of hair and hers was too short to make it look right. In the end, Kate's mother tracked down a beauty shop near the harbor that provided a crown of fake curls that closely matched Kate's hair.

The two rooms occupied by the bride looked like a tornado had passed through it. Kim and her bridesmaids had created a maze of ironing boards, makeup cases and sandwich wrappers. The sandwiches had been ordered from the same sub place where Kate had bought dinner to take back to the cottage Friday night.

Despite the frenzy around her, she had moments when thoughts of Hugh would override everything, and she'd wonder how he was spending his day. Then Harry called to ask when the flowers were supposed to arrive, and that's how Kate learned that Hugh was hosting a pizza and beer party for the guys down at the cottage.

It sounded way too jolly to suit Kate, considering the moody person who had stomped out of the cottage early that morning. It looked as if Hugh was one of those guys who wasn't very in touch with his feelings. So what else was new?

Kate vowed to put him out of her mind completely. Besides helping Kim get beautiful for the big moment, she dashed around taking candid shots of the preparations. Yes, there would be formal pictures arranged by the wedding photographer, even informal ones taken at the reception. But Kate knew the kind of memories she wanted to capture for her sister, and her trusty little camera was going everywhere with her today. Besides, concentrating on photography turned out to be the best way to forget about the rat from Hollywood.

About thirty minutes before they were scheduled to leave the Townsend House for Belcourt Castle, Ruth's sister, Andrea, arrived with Gillian, the flower girl. From the moment Gillian dashed into the room, Kate knew why Andrea had waited until the last minute to bring her. She was a whirlwind of activity in a room that didn't need an ounce more of confusion.

She had a small bandage around her ankle under the lace-trimmed socks she wore, but that was the only evidence that she'd sprained her ankle the day before. A slight injury wasn't keeping this girl out of the lineup, and Kate smiled, remembering how impatient she'd always been with any restraint on her freedom.

Gillian didn't want to sit still long enough to have a little makeup applied to her skinned nose, let alone have her black curls arranged by the hairdresser. Kate decided to amuse her by taking countless pictures during the process.

"So many pictures!" Gillian laughed, her dimples flashing. But she obviously loved being the one constantly in Kate's viewfinder.

"Can you say *modeling career*?" Ruth murmured to Andrea.

"Not docile enough," Andrea, also a dark-haired beauty, murmured back.

"What's *docile*?" Gillian wiggled on the chair while the hairdresser struggled to attach a wreath of flowers to her head.

"It means quiet," Kate said as she moved around the beautiful child, snapping away. She'd always felt a connection with this vibrant kid, but even more so today. Half a roll of film later, she figured out why. Gillian's blue eyes and black hair reminded her of Hugh. If he had a little girl she might look very much like this one.

"I *hate* being quiet," Gillian said.

"Don't we know it," Andrea said.

"Well, nobody has to be quiet in this room," Kim said. She stood nearby while her mother carefully powdered her nose so as not to get any on the vintage white lace.

Kate took a quick shot of that. For a casual person

who usually cared little about how she looked, Kim made an amazingly regal bride. During the reception she might kick off her shoes and rub off most of the makeup her mother had carefully applied, but for the moment, she'd been transformed into a goddess. Kate blinked away proud tears.

"Do I gotta be quiet in the church?" Gillian asked.

Kim glanced at her. "Belcourt isn't exactly a ch—"

"Close enough," Andrea said. "And Gillian understands that we all have to be very, very quiet in church, don't we, Gillian?"

"I understand, but I *hate* that."

"The wedding will be over before you know it," Kate told her. "Then we'll have the party, and I promise lots of guys will want to dance with you." Silly as the idea was, she'd decided to make sure that Hugh danced with Gillian at least once. Kate would be nearby, with her camera. Food for her fantasies. The way things were going, she'd have to live on them for a long time.

"Dancing!" Gillian threw her arms in the air and the hairdresser had to duck to keep from getting socked in the face. "Dancing's cool!"

"She's precious," Emily Cooper murmured, longing in her voice.

Kate swallowed a lump in her throat. Lack of sleep and the pressure of her sister's wedding must be making her weepy. The longer she looked at Gillian, the more she imagined what it would be like to have a child of her own some day.

She'd never considered it before. She'd been quite willing to let Kim and Stuart produce grandchildren for her mom and dad to spoil. In her view, the biological clock concept was a Madison Avenue plot to sell diapers and strollers.

Apparently not entirely. If Gillian hadn't been dressed in a frothy lace dress and recently had her hair meticulously styled, Kate would have scooped her up and given her a bear hug. She'd never felt such a strong urge before. Maybe after the wedding it would go away. She hoped so, because, unlike Kim, she had no groom in sight.

At last everyone was ready to go.

"Even Kate!" Bette teased.

"I promised, didn't I?" She'd surprised herself by not feeling the need to add excitement to the event by dawdling and then having to rush. Funny, but ever since meeting Hugh, she'd lost the desire to do that. With Hugh around, her life had plenty of drama.

By the time the bride and her entourage ventured downstairs, Stuart, his family, and the groomsmen had already left the Townsend House. Outside, a white stretch limo waited at the curb. Emily and John had hired the sleek vehicle, over Kim's protests, to transport the bridal party to Belcourt Castle.

Although Kim thought the limo was a waste of money, Kate loved the concept and had convinced Kim to go along. Kate suspected that their parents felt a little guilty about not being around for the work of planning the wedding. After the scrimping she and Kim had done to put on this first-rate wedding in a month's time, Kate thought they deserved a ride in a limo.

She ended up being first out the door of the inn, with Gillian holding fast to her hand. The little girl stopped dead in her tracks when she caught sight of the long limo. Maybe because Kate had promised her dancing at the party, she seemed to think that Kate was the keeper of all important information. She looked up at Kate, her eyes wide. "What *is* that big thing?"

"It's called a limousine," Kate said. "Special people get to ride around in it."

"Oh, my gosh. Is Barbie in there?"

Kate managed to keep a straight face. "No, not this time."

Gillian thought about that for a moment. "So I guess *we* get to be the special people!" With that she let go of Kate's hand and marched to the door the limo driver held open. Then she turned and blew everyone a kiss before stepping inside.

It was the kind of silliness they all needed. Kim, especially, had been getting way too serious, and now she laughed. "She caught on to that pretty fast."

"She catches on to everything fast." Andrea hurried after her daughter. "And now I'd better get to her before she discovers the wet bar."

Kate's dad took charge of getting the wedding bouquets loaded into the trunk of the limo while Kate's mom shepherded everyone inside the car. After a little jockeying and arranging of long skirts, they were all cocooned within the plush interior and began the short drive to Belcourt Castle.

"It's just like prom, minus the dates!" Ruth said.

"Good riddance to those dates," Bette said. "That was the worst night of my life. In case you're forgotten, Donald Hynes spent the entire evening demonstrating how he could belch the fight song."

"And Horace Wimpleton, my wonderful date, took his trig book along to cram for a test," Sabrina said.

Then the race was on to see who'd had the worst

prom experience, the worst date ever, the most horrible first date, the most humiliating breakup. Kate's parents joined in the laughter and teasing because they'd been there through it all as this crowd of girls slowly became women. Kate longed to freeze the action and keep them right in this moment for a little longer. But she couldn't, so she started snapping pictures.

First she concentrated on her parents, her mother so young and vibrant, her father basking in the role of being the only man in the midst of a bevy of finely turned-out women. Then she took pictures of Kim, a bride beautiful enough to bring fresh tears to her eyes. Finally she turned her camera toward her buddies. If only their long-suffering teachers and principals could see them now. In fact, a couple of them would be there, she remembered, thinking of the guest list.

Each of her friends, independent thinkers all, had been allowed to choose her own dress and color so long as the result was vintage and lacy. Ruth was in pale blue, Sabrina in dusty rose and Bette in pale yellow. The women all had a certain luster about them, as if they knew the importance of today. Kim was the first of the gang to get married, and after this their group of five would never be quite the same.

As long as everyone stayed in the limo, they were caught in time, full of giddy anticipation that buoyed them up and made their faces glow. Kate realized that was why she took pictures in the first place—to record moments like this, real moments, not the arranged production of glamour shots in the studio. And when this wedding was over and the dust had settled, she'd have to tell her father and Kim that she needed to take a leave of absence from Cooper Photography. Perhaps daring to do what she had the night before had given her the courage for this bold step.

The decision left her a little breathless. There was one person she could tell now, one person who would understand and support her plan. But she wouldn't tell him, because her mental health required that she stay far away from Hugh Armstrong.

As luck would have it, Hugh was stationed at the head of the walkway leading up to the imposing mansion. Harry must have asked him to watch for them and escort them all to the proper place. Everything about this building was proper. Kate wondered if Kim was having second thoughts about canceling the rehearsal.

Kate was having second thoughts about her ability to stay away from Hugh. The sight of him in a tux was enough to rattle the composure of any woman. If he hadn't kicked her out of his cottage early this morning, she'd be making plans to seduce him on the grounds of Belcourt Castle.

But he had kicked her out, so she'd eat dirt before she'd allow herself to chase after him. Damn, he looked good though, with his broad shoulders straining the seams of his jacket and his eyes even more blue than she remembered. Belcourt was more of an elaborate mansion than an actual castle, but Hugh still looked like the prince of her dreams standing there with the elegant structure in the background. Fortunately she didn't look too bad, herself. She hoped he would get an eyeful of her in her mint-green vintage lace dress and regret his boorish behavior.

Maybe after watching her for a little while tonight, he'd beg for another chance to continue their affair.

She wouldn't agree to anything, of course. He was bad for her, and she needed to remember that.

Still, it would be sweet to listen to him beg.

HUGH SUSPECTED HARRY of making him the limo reception guy on purpose. Harry would be trying to throw him in Kate's path whenever possible. He couldn't refuse to escort the bridal party into the chambers reserved for them without seeming like a grouch, and he didn't want to put a damper on Stuart's wedding. So he'd agreed.

But the minute Kate stepped out of the limo looking like a princess in her mint-green outfit, he felt a sharp pain in the region of his heart. She had no business looking so gorgeous. She wasn't supposed to outshine the bride.

Stuart wouldn't agree with him that Kate was the more beautiful, of course, but Hugh was entitled to his opinion. Kim was a knockout, though, he had to admit as she climbed carefully out of the car.

Because she was Kate's twin, he had no trouble imagining how Kate would look in a wedding dress, and that caused him another sharp pain of regret. Kate would marry someone eventually, maybe even one of the single guys attending this wedding. She'd grown up in Providence, so she had plenty of old friends, even old flames.

The thought gave him heartburn. "If everyone will follow me, I'll show you where you're supposed to hang out until the procession begins," he said as the bridesmaids were handed one by one out of the car by the limo driver.

"I'm Gillian. I'm the flower girl." A dark-haired little cherub skipped over to him and grabbed his hand as the women stood around smoothing their outfits and straightening the flowers in their hair.

"So I heard." God, she was cute. And according to Stuart, she had a personality to match Kate's. Looking at her he could imagine what Kate was like as a kid, only with carrot-red hair instead of glossy black.

But he couldn't get too wrapped up in this little sweetie. As the person in charge of meeting the limo, he had duties. He glanced back to where Kate's dad and the limo driver were taking colorful bouquets out of the trunk. "You guys need any help with that?"

"Thanks, but we've got it." John's tone was pleasant enough, but he still seemed suspicious of Hugh. "Lead the way, and we'll be behind you."

"Let's lead the way!" Gillian cried, swinging his hand back and forth. "I like that."

"Okay." He glanced around at the assembled women. "Everybody all set?"

"All set," Kim said.

"Then, let's—"

"Mister Man, can I ride on your shoulders?"

"Gillian," said a dark-haired woman who was obviously the little girl's mother. "I don't—"

"We'll be real careful of my pretty clothes, won't we?" She gazed up at Hugh with her china-doll eyes.

He melted. Not many people knew he was a sucker for kids, especially little girls. He glanced over at Gillian's mom. "Might not be a bad idea for her to be up off the sidewalk to protect that white dress. And I will be careful."

"Thank you. We haven't met." The woman stepped closer and offered her hand. "I'm Andrea Jacobs, Gillian's mother."

"I'm Hugh Armstrong, the best man's brother."

"The stuntman." Andrea smiled as she clasped his hand.

"A *stuntman*?" Gillian asked. "What's that?"

"I do tricks." The warmth of Andrea's smile and her handshake warned him to take a quick look at her left hand. No wedding ring. Probably no husband around. He'd better be careful. His natural fondness for kids could get him in trouble, as he'd discovered several times with single mothers.

Besides, he felt Kate's eyes burning a hole in his back. She was the type to notice, and he didn't plan to rub salt in her wounds by seeming to be interested in another woman.

"I wanna see some tricks," Gillian said.

"Okay, I'll show you how I can be an elevator." He released Andrea's hand quickly and crouched down to Gillian's level. "Elevator going up."

"Yay!" Gillian clapped her hands and started to scramble onto his back.

"Easy!" He grasped her gently around the waist, marveling at how small and light she was. "Let me carry you on one shoulder, so we don't muss up your dress." Without waiting for her agreement, he settled her on his left shoulder and rose partway. "First floor!"

"Ding, ding!" Gillian pushed on his nose.

He stood erect and could have sworn he heard the click of a camera and the soft whir of an automatic rewind. "Second floor!" But when he looked over at Kate, she had no camera in her hands. She did have a little beaded bag, however, and it was big enough to hold her tiny thirty-five millimeter. He'd bet he'd guessed right.

He was a little confused about why she'd want to

waste film on him, though. Maybe she was only interested in Gillian, and he happened to be in the way.
That was okay. He could understand why Kate would
want about a thousand pictures of the little girl. He
wouldn't mind having a few, himself.

"Now I'll show you how I can be a train," Hugh
said to Gillian. As he started forward, he made chug-
ging noises and blew through his free hand to make a
sound like a train whistle.

"Look at these big trees!" Gillian said.

"Don't even think about it, girl," Andrea said. She
glanced over at Hugh. "Did you hear about the tree-
climbing incident yesterday?"

"I did, as a matter of fact."

Andrea lowered her voice. "She's a handful. Thank
you for helping."

"My pleasure." He knew about kids like this. He
used to be one. He still was, in a way.

"Toot, toot!" Gillian yelled, pulling on Hugh's ear.

This time he caught Kate taking a picture. "Fill up
that portfolio," he called to her.

Her mother turned to Kate. "What portfolio?"

Hugh could have kicked himself. She wasn't announcing her intentions to her family, and he knew
that. "A wedding portfolio for Kim and Stuart is what
I meant," Hugh said.

"Oh! Well, that's very nice," Emily said.

"I wanted to bring my camera," John said from the
rear of the procession. "But I couldn't figure out
where to put it. The father of the bride doesn't carry a
purse."

"That's okay, Dad." Kate was shooting pictures
openly now, lifting the hem of her skirt with one hand

and snapping shots of the procession with the other. "Once the wedding's over, you can borrow mine."

"When the wedding's over, we're gonna *party!*" Gillian said. Then she pulled on Hugh's ear again. "Will you dance with me?"

"You bet."

"Little girls have an advantage," Andrea said quietly. "They don't think to be shy."

Hugh's heart squeezed. Andrea wanted to be promised a dance, too. "I'm going to dance with as many beautiful women as I can tonight," Hugh said. And that would probably convince Kate he was a total jerk. Maybe that was for the best. But he'd be damned if he'd lead Andrea on and risk hurting someone else. "Then tomorrow it's straight back to California for me."

"Oh." Andrea's voice betrayed her disappointment. "That's too bad."

"It's my life. I'm constantly on the go, and that's the way I like it—free as a bird." The words tasted bitter on his tongue. His type of freedom meant he'd never carry his own child on his shoulder or stand at the end of the aisle and watch a redheaded beauty come toward him in a white dress. He didn't want that kind of freedom anymore, but he, the daredevil who leaped from burning buildings and swam through rapids, was afraid to reach out for what he wanted.

He escorted the bridal party into the elegant antechamber adjacent to the French Gothic ballroom where guests were gathering. Reluctantly he lowered Gillian to the carpet and promised her as many dances as she wanted during the party. The thought came to mind that Gillian might be the only female in the vicinity he could relate to without danger. She was a creature of the moment, not worried about next week or next year, when he would be gone.

He used to be like that. He'd love to blame the transformation on Kate and her cozy family and the trappings of this warm and wonderful wedding. He'd love to, but he couldn't. Life as he knew it hadn't been working for quite a while, and it had taken someone as vibrant and non-Hollywood as Kate to make him realize that he needed to make a change.

But his discovery was too new and untried for him to act on it. Before trying to find a woman to share his life with, he had to decide what kind of life that would be. Maybe it was time to stop risking his safety in front of the camera and see what he could do behind it. After making hundreds of movies, he had a pretty good idea of what constituted a good one.

And after fifteen years in Hollywood he'd made the right connections to get financial backing, especially if he found a decent script. He knew who would work cheap and who liked the idea of taking a chance on an independent venture. The more he thought about it, the more excited he became.

That was a huge switch for him to make, though, and he needed to make it alone so that if it went sour he didn't take anyone down with him. Especially someone like Kate. Before he left the chamber to go check on Stuart and Harry, he took one last look at Kate flitting around with her camera constantly clicking.

She reminded him of an exotic butterfly, and the overwhelming emotions he felt every time he saw her or even thought about her boiled down to one inescapable realization. He'd fallen in love with her. The timing for such an emotion to grab him was terrible. And as he knew from years in the movie business, timing was everything.

14

KATE COULDN'T IMAGINE a more perfect wedding. Late afternoon sun filtered through the stained glass windows of the French Gothic ballroom and cast jeweled light on two hundred and twenty guests seated beneath the room's vaulted ceilings. Candlelight flickering at the altar and the sparkling light of four massive chandeliers turned the room into a fairyland.

Despite skipping the rehearsal, the wedding party had moved through the processional without incident. Even little Gillian seemed subdued by the wonder of it all. After strewing her basket of rose petals and waving at the guests like a homecoming queen on a float, she'd returned to her mother's lap and stayed there, much to Kate's amazement. Kate had followed Gillian's lead and decided to be circumspect, herself. She'd tucked her camera away until after the recessional.

At the focal point of all this majesty stood Kim and Stuart, proudly repeating the time-honored vows of marriage. As they pledged to love each other forever in voices firm with conviction, Kate sent up a prayer of gratitude for whoever had invented waterproof mascara.

She was so happy for Kim. So unbelievably happy. But now she knew that she wanted this, too, wanted the handsome prince and the adorable children and the promise of a love everlasting. She wanted it so much that her whole body ached.

Her mother might say it was the twin syndrome kicking in. The sisters had passed through the stages of life so closely bonded that Kim's marriage would naturally signal Kate's readiness to do likewise. Kate thought it might also have something to do with her near-miss this weekend. If Hugh had turned out to be the person she'd thought on Friday night, they might already be planning their wedding.

But Hugh wasn't the man she'd thought he was. He couldn't even be her faux hero for a weekend without chickening out when a nightmare threatened his masculine pride. Therefore she needed to forget about Hugh and open herself to the possibility of another man, maybe even some man in this room.

Unfortunately she knew just about every single guy within these massive walls, and only one made her heart beat faster—the one she'd vowed to forget. She knew exactly where he was sitting on the groom's side of the aisle. From the corner of her eye she could see him, his dark hair gleaming in the light from the chandelier over his head.

Andrea wanted him, too. And then there was Temple, Stuart's sister, who had maneuvered things so that she was sitting next to him. From what Kate had seen of Temple's tactics, she was probably pressing her thigh against Hugh's by now. The reception would turn into a free-for-all as women flocked to dance with the handsome stranger from California, a man who'd been the stand-in for Antonio Banderas, for God's sake.

Kate figured she'd let them all find out for themselves that Hugh was beautiful to look at and impossible to hold. All except Andrea, who'd already been hurt once and didn't deserve another slap in the face. Kate planned to have a talk with Andrea and steer her toward Harry. The more she thought about it, the more she thought Andrea and Harry would be perfect for each other.

Logically, even Kate should be interested in Harry, who was a quieter, gentler version of Hugh. But that's how it was with chemistry. Either it was there or it wasn't, and Harry didn't do a thing for her. Too bad Mister Hollywood did.

"You may kiss the bride," said Reverend Applegate.

Stuart lifted Kim's lace veil and kissed her so ardently that Kate was shocked. Maybe there was more drama in that relationship than she'd thought. She took a chance and looked in Hugh's direction. He was gazing right back at her, his jaw set, his blue eyes intense.

Talk about chemistry. She could feel it pulsing between them all the way across the room. Her heartbeat quickened. He still wanted her, even though he'd obviously tried to put her out of his mind. With luck, memories of her would haunt him for a while after he went back to California.

Yeah, maybe for all of two weeks. Men like Hugh didn't stay lonely for long.

The guests broke into applause as Reverend Applegate presented the newly married couple, and once again Kate found herself with a lump in her throat that was part happiness and part envy. Kim and Stuart walked down the long aisle accompanied by deep-throated organ music. Kate couldn't ask for anything more dramatic and thrilling, except for Hugh to be the one who offered his arm to her instead of Harry.

"Are you okay?" Harry murmured as they followed Stuart and Kim toward the door at the back of the room.

Kate swallowed. "Uh-huh. This is an emotional moment, that's all."

"I'm sure it is. But...let me know if there's anything...anything I can do."

She wondered how much Harry knew. He and Hugh were twins, after all, and Kate had firsthand knowledge of the psychic link that often existed between twins. "Thanks," she said. "I will." When they were almost out the door, she thought of a way he could help her. "There is something I'd like to ask," she said softly.

"What?"

"Who's Joe?"

The muscles in Harry's arm stiffened. "He was our brother."

"Was?"

"He died in a car accident when Hugh and I were seventeen."

HUGH DIDN'T KNOW IF HE was supposed to be with the wedding party as they gathered in the mansion's inner courtyard for pictures. Most likely he was expected to join the other guests assembling for dinner in the Italian Banquet Hall. But he couldn't help himself. He was drawn to Kate as if she'd attached a leash to his starched collar and was pulling him along with her wherever she went.

He was fascinated with her graceful movements in the green lace dress, an outfit so different from the type she usually wore, yet so perfect for her, too. Her skinny tops and tight capris expressed the rebel in her, but this dress revealed her more traditional side. That normally hidden part of her personality had kept her in Providence working in her dad's photo studio, even though she was becoming bored. And tradition had played a part in her wanting a heroic man to marry.

She deserved that, and he wanted her to be happy. Even if it killed him.

The courtyard, open to the sky but surrounded on all sides by wings of the huge mansion, was a flurry of activity. Gillian ran happily in and out of the shrubbery, obviously thrilled to be released from quiet time. Andrea tried to keep her corralled so she'd look decent for the pictures, but Hugh could see that would be a losing effort. The little girl had made it through the ceremony, but that was going to be the extent of her good behavior. Even Hugh ran out of ideas for keeping her entertained while the adults wrangled about the arrangement of the shots.

As Hugh had predicted, the photograph-savvy Coopers had the poor wedding photographer wringing his hands as they insisted on directing the action. Emily tried to make peace, but Kim, Kate, John and Nick all had opinions about how the poses should be set up. They disagreed with the photographer and they disagreed with each other.

"Didn't you and Nick work this all out today?" an exasperated looking Emily said to her husband.

"Yeah, but the light's different. Plus we're losing our light by the minute!" John said. "Then we'll have to start filling in with flash, and I don't like having to—"

"Flash is the only way to go," Nick said.

"No, we definitely need umbrella lights, and I don't know why we didn't just do that in the first place." Kim leaned against her new groom. "And in about five minutes I'm going to take off my shoes, so we'll have to skip the full-length shots after that."

Kate had her own little camera in motion again, capturing the brouhaha on film. "Why won't anybody listen to my idea of having Kim and Stuart pose in the branches of that tree?" she asked. "And barefoot would be awesome. We really should have gone down to Gooseberry Beach. It's not that far."

Hugh had to smile at that one. Typical of her to want the wedding party to start climbing trees and playing in the waves for a little drama.

Finally they assembled the group against a background that John and Nick could both agree on. The photographer had completely lost control of the situation and was simply following orders.

"We don't have our flower girl," Kate said. "Where's Gillian?"

"She's over here, but I can't guarantee how clean she'll be," Andrea said. "We may have to airbrush out some dirt stains. Gillian, come out from behind that bush, right now."

"Come out, come out, wherever you are!" Kate called.

Everyone waited, but Gillian didn't appear.

Hugh walked over to the hedge and pushed aside the thick branches, expecting to see Gillian hiding behind them. She wasn't there. "She must have gone somewhere else."

Frowning, Andrea hurried toward the bush. "I could have sworn that's where she went."

"Well, she's not there now." Hugh started searching behind all the bushes and before long so did everyone else. The courtyard echoed with the sound of the little girl's name being called over and over.

"Okay, Gillian," Andrea said. "This isn't funny. Come on out."

"I don't dance with girls who hide and scare people," Hugh said.

Kate walked over to them, alarm in her green eyes. "I don't think she's here."

"Of course she is," Andrea said. "She was just—"

"Kate's right," Hugh said, putting himself in Gillian's place. "She got bored with the delay and she's gone off on some adventure."

"Exactly," Kate said, meeting his gaze.

"Just like you would," he said.

"And you."

"So where do you think?" Hugh asked. But even as he asked the question, he knew. The girl was a climber, and they'd passed some beauties on the way into the castle. Gillian had even commented on the tall trees. Very tall trees. His stomach pitched. "Out in front," he said.

"Let's go." Kate headed toward the nearest doorway.

"Faster," Hugh said, coming up behind her. "Maybe we can catch her before she gets too high."

"Right." Kate pulled open the door, lifted her skirts and ran across the hallway to the majestic front door of the mansion.

Hugh followed, with Andrea close behind and the rest of the wedding party hot on her heels.

"She can't be out there," Andrea protested. "That door's too heavy for her to open."

"She just waited until somebody else opened it and

then she slipped out," Kate called over her shoulder. "I used to do it all the time."

"Oh, God," Andrea wailed. "You think she climbed one of those trees, don't you?"

Hugh didn't take time to answer. He barreled out the front door. Calling Gillian's name wasn't necessary. She was already yelling her head off as she clung to one of the top branches of a giant oak. She looked so tiny up there, like someone's doll stuck in the branches. And she would break like one if she fell from that height. He estimated she was at least thirty feet off the ground.

"I can't get down!" she cried. "Somebody help! Please help!" Then she began to cry.

"We're coming," Kate said. "It's okay, Gillian. You'll be fine!"

"Oh, dear Lord!" Andrea started toward the tree, fancy dress and all, as if she meant to climb right up to where her child was stranded.

"Hold on, Andrea. I'll get her." Hugh whipped off his tux jacket. "Kate, keep talking to her." He'd been in movies where someone was in danger of falling from a ledge, or a character had to jump from a burning building. What the hell had the script called for in that situation? Then he remembered. "Somebody go find a blanket, the biggest one you can come up with."

"I will!" Kim said, and ran off towards the mansion, her skirts and veil flying.

"Harry, you and Stuart organize the men to hold the blanket like a net under the tree." He hoped the net wouldn't be tested. If it was, he hoped it worked like it did in the movies.

Kate started coaxing Gillian to sing. "Let's do 'Row, Row, Row Your Boat,'" she said.

"I don't wanna!"

"Come on. I'll start." Kate started belting out the tune, and soon everybody joined in except Andrea and Gillian.

Hugh took a moment to put a hand on Andrea's arm and give it a reassuring squeeze. "Listen, don't worry. I've been in hundreds of situations like this. Gillian will be fine."

She spoke through colorless lips. "But...it was pretend."

"It was real enough for me." Then he headed for the tree. As he climbed, Kate lead the group below in "I'm a Little Teapot." But Gillian was too scared to sing. She just kept on crying. Hugh talked to her, too, trying to be reassuring. He sure hoped Kate would stay away from "Rock-a-bye Baby."

The singing was a good idea, but it wasn't working. Hugh was afraid if Gillian got much more hysterical she wouldn't be willing to let go of the branch long enough to grab on to him. A breeze rustled the leaves and swayed the branch Gillian was clutching so desperately. She screamed.

"It's okay, Gillian," he said. "I'm almost there."

She continued to sob. He could see her tear-stained face through the leaves, and she was one miserable little wood sprite. She was also holding on to that branch for dear life. If he couldn't get her to lighten up he'd have a hell of a time prying her loose.

Then a scene from another movie flashed into his mind. He didn't remember the details, except the distraught character had been calmed by having her picture taken by a roving photographer. It was a thought.

"Kate?" he called down.

"I'm a Little Teapot" came to a halt.

"What?" she asked.

"Do you still have your camera?"

"Um, yeah. Why?"

"Take some pictures of Gillian so she can be famous, okay?"

Gillian stopped crying for the first time since he'd started up the tree. "F-famous?" she said, sniffing.

"You bet! Everybody will want a picture of the girl who climbed up in this tree."

"Famous like B-barbie?"

"Absolutely!"

"Hey, Gillian!" Kate said. "I've got you in my sights, girl, and you look mahvelous!" Kate's flash went off. "Now I'll try it from another angle. You are going to be so famous!"

"I am?"

"Of course! How many kids have a picture of themselves in a big tree?"

"Nobody," came the trembling little voice. "Can you take some more pictures?"

"Watch me. I'll take the whole roll."

The knot of tension eased in Hugh's stomach. He started out on the branch toward Gillian, inching carefully and listening for any crackling sound that would mean too much stress. If the branch gave way...

But it held. He reached out and wrapped his hand around her tiny arm.

"Time to go back, kiddo," he said.

Gillian stared down at Kate snapping pictures below her. "Can't."

Uh-oh. She was frozen with fear, after all. "Sure, you can," he coaxed. "Just grab hold of me. Simple."

"No, I mean I can't because Kate's still taking pictures."

He almost laughed. "Oh." He was pretty sure Kate had finished the roll by now and was using the flash to simulate taking more shots. "Kate? You about done?"

"Uh, yeah! One more."

Her camera flashed, and he looked away so it wouldn't affect his vision.

"That's it," Kate said. "You can come on down now, Gillian."

"Okay."

Hugh couldn't believe how easy it was after that. Carrying a little kid like Gillian down from a tree was about ten times more comfortable than hauling adults through heavy waves. When he neared the bottom, the men rushed forward and helped him the rest of the way. Eager hands lifted Gillian from his arms and transferred her to Andrea.

Then everyone crowded around him, clapping him on the back and offering congratulations, which surprised the hell out of him.

"No big deal," he said, meaning it. In the life of a stuntman, this was puppy chow. They wanted to make him out as some sort of hero, but they didn't understand how easy it was. They gave him all the credit for the picture-taking idea, too. He tried to tell them it wasn't his brainstorm, that it had come from a movie. Nobody seemed to care.

The lavish praise threw him for a loop. In his world, the stars got all the attention. Throughout the dinner and the dancing afterward, everyone treated him like a star, everyone except the one person he wanted to fawn over him. For some strange reason, although this appeared to be his moment of glory, Kate kept her distance.

THE MOMENT HUGH HAD started up the tree, Kate had finally admitted the truth. He was the hero she'd been looking for, and she was desperately in love with him. After her brief talk with Harry right after the ceremony, she also knew her love was hopeless. Harry had explained how the death of their brother had scarred them both. Rationally they knew that loving someone didn't mean that person would die, but emotionally...that was a different story.

Harry said he'd become a doctor in an attempt to face down the specter of death, while Hugh had become a stuntman so he could take death-defying risks all the time. Neither of them had ever sustained a relationship with a woman for longer than a few weeks.

Although Harry had urged Kate to pursue his brother, he couldn't know how completely Hugh had rejected her after waking from his nightmare of Joe. Hugh didn't want her, didn't want the possible pain that coming out of his shell would cause. Loving him, she would respect that. She wasn't about to try and change him for his own good. He was a grown man, and he knew how he wanted to live by now. So...she'd let him go.

In the beginning of the evening she found it easy to avoid him. He was the man of the hour and surrounded by a crowd of people all the time. Andrea obviously worshipped him, and she'd given him a heartfelt hug before taking Gillian home after dinner. Kate had felt no jealousy watching the embrace. She couldn't be jealous of anyone, knowing that no woman would ever hold Hugh for long. It didn't matter who he spent time with during the reception.

She just didn't want him to spend time with her. It would hurt too much. Consequently, whenever she saw him coming in her direction, she found an excuse to slip away.

If this were a movie, she would win the bridal bouquet toss and Hugh would snag the garter, and that would bring them together in spite of themselves. Hugh would have a sudden change of heart, and they would live happily ever after. But this wasn't a movie, Kate reminded herself, and she didn't even try very hard for the bouquet. Temple, Stuart's sister, caught it instead.

Hugh didn't get the garter, either. It went to Harry. Kate wondered if Harry would break the pattern he and Hugh had established and eventually find a woman to love. She thought he might, because at least he was focusing on the problem. Hugh didn't want to think about it, much less take a chance on loving someone.

The evening became an endurance test. Much as she wanted Kim and Stuart to enjoy themselves at their wedding reception, she hoped they'd take their leave soon. The guests were having a wonderful time and nobody would go home until the bride and groom made their exit. Finally, that moment came.

Armed with tiny containers of bubbles, the guests poured out through the same heavy doorway Gillian had used to make her escape hours earlier. As Kate looked up at the tree looming in the darkness, she thought of how she'd misjudged Hugh's hero potential. After today, she had no doubt he'd leap on a live grenade in a foxhole.

She'd found her hero, but she hadn't been specific enough when she'd made her wish. She'd forgotten to add that the man of her dreams had to be free to give her his heart. Hugh was chained by tragic memories.

Kim and Stuart came through the door and ran a gauntlet of bubbles that sparkled in the moonlight. Hopping into Stuart's car, they drove away to a chorus of goodbyes and well-wishes. The wedding was over.

As the guests returned to the ballroom, Kate lingered a moment, gazing up at the almost full moon. She felt an arm around her waist and turned to find her mother standing next to her.

"It was beautiful, wasn't it?" her mother said, wiping at her eyes.

Kate slipped an arm around her mother's waist and hugged her back. "Yes, it was, Mom. Beautiful."

Her mother smiled. "Not every wedding has a rescue as part of the program."

"Nope." Kate managed a smile of her own. So far her parents had been too busy to quiz her about Hugh.

"I haven't seen you with him tonight. Is something wrong?"

So the wedding was over and Emily could turn her attention to her other daughter. Kate didn't feel up to dodging questions. "Nothing's wrong," she said. "You know how it is. After that first infatuation, you find out you're all wrong for each other."

"I don't believe that for a minute. I already told your father that this man is the first one I've seen who wouldn't bore you to tears."

Kate sighed. "Mom, he's going back to California tomorrow, and that's the end of that."

Kate's mother leveled a direct gaze at her and said, "Go with him."

KATE STARED AT HER MOTHER.

"You heard me. Go with him. Try out the lifestyle. Look into becoming a freelance photographer. And don't tell me you haven't been thinking about it. You've stuck with the studio longer than I ever thought you would."

"What are you talking about?" Kate felt her cheeks growing hot. She might have decided to take a leave of absence, but she wanted to announce that on her schedule. "I love the studio!"

"You love your father and Kim. You didn't want to hurt them by striking out on your own. I've known that for a long time. So has your dad."

Kate was speechless. And scared. Her mother had just opened the cage door, and although Kate had started planning her flight to freedom, she didn't know if she was ready to begin right this minute.

Emily gave her an affectionate squeeze. "You can leave town without feeling guilty, by the way. I checked with Nick, and he's agreed to hang around and mind the place for a while. Your dad will make sure he's familiar with everything before we go back to Florida. Fly back with Hugh. Call it a long-overdue vacation."

"We're talking about two different things here,

Mom. My taking a break from studio photography has nothing to do with going to California."

"I think combining the two would be brilliant."

Kate sighed. "Aren't you forgetting something? Hugh hasn't asked me to go to California with him."

"Have you given him the chance?"

"No." She didn't want to tell her mother about the humiliating episode in which Hugh had practically ordered her out of his bedroom, but that might be the only way her mother would understand that Hugh wasn't in the market for a traveling companion.

"Talk with him, Kate. I have."

"You?" Kate wondered how in the world she'd missed seeing that.

"Well, of course I've talked with him. First of all I needed to thank him for saving the day. That gave me a chance to find out a little more about him. Did you know he's thinking of giving up being a stuntman and going into directing?"

Dazed, Kate shook her head.

"Talk to him," Emily said. "I've figured out that you two had some sort of disagreement, but I think he wants to make amends."

Or he wants to ask for one more night before he leaves. Whatever Hugh's motivation, she was beginning to understand her mother's. Emily had wedding fever. She'd married off one daughter, and now she was ready to start on the second one. Hugh was the last person she'd seen Kate kissing, so he was the logical candidate. He'd also conducted himself like a hero today, and no woman was immune to that.

"We'll see," she said to placate her mother. Then she took a deep breath. "Right now, I could use a walk on Gooseberry Beach."

Emily studied her for a few seconds. "Good idea. Why don't you ask Hugh if he wants to go?"

"I want to go alone, Mom."

Her mother sighed. "You're being difficult."

Kate laughed and gave her mom another hug. "So what's new about that?"

"How long will you be?"

"Not long. Give me a half hour. I'll bet it'll take at least that long for this party to wind down. And I need—"

"I understand, sweetie. Your sister just got married and I've given you permission to be yourself for a change. That's a lot to digest. Go on. Walk on the beach. Think about what I said."

"I'm not going to California, but I might get into that freelance thing."

Her mother nodded. "Good. You'd be terrific. You and Nick are more alike than you think."

"Maybe, but I can wait until after Kim comes back from her honeymoon. Nick doesn't have to rearrange his life for me."

"We'll see. We can talk about it tomorrow."

"All right." *After Hugh leaves*, she amended silently. Until she knew he was gone, really gone, she wouldn't be able to concentrate on anything. "And do *not* find Hugh and send him after me, okay?"

"Okay."

With a quick wave to her mother, Kate took the route she and Kim had scoped out one day when they'd thought about taking wedding pictures on the beach. They'd abandoned the idea as using up too much time, but Kate still thought it would've been cool.

If they'd taken pictures on the beach, Gillian

wouldn't have climbed the tree. But she would have found something else to get into, Kate thought with a smile. She was starting to appreciate how much trouble she'd caused as a kid, and how tolerant her parents had been. They still were. Although they would dearly love for her to stay with Kim and run the studio, they were encouraging her to leave.

It was fitting that they'd do something like that. They were the ones who'd taught her that love meant allowing people to be themselves, and that was why she wouldn't even consider foisting herself off on Hugh. She couldn't have the relationship she wanted without Hugh changing, and she wouldn't ask him to do that. No matter how much she ached whenever she thought of never seeing him again, it was the right way to treat the person you loved.

Moonlight and the sound of lapping waves guided her to the beach. Once she reached the sand, she glanced around to make sure the place was deserted. Then she took off her shoes and reached under her skirt to strip off her panty hose. Stuffing them in the toe of one shoe, she started down the beach, her bare feet sinking into the cool sand.

The moon traced a path across the water, and she longed for a camera. But to capture the moonlight on the water, she'd need more than her little thirty-five millimeter. This shot required a tripod and a long exposure. She stood there digging her toes into the sand while she planned how she'd do it.

If she gave up studio photography, she could spend all kinds of time with shots like this. Her savings would take her for six months, longer if she scrimped. Surely in that time she'd be able to sell some pictures.

She already had a list of magazines which might be interested.

This was a move she'd been dreaming about for a long time. Once she got past this business with Hugh, she'd appreciate the opportunity more. She'd celebrate her new independence and take a little more pride in her newfound bravery. And she would get over Hugh. She would.

"What I wouldn't give to be out on the water tonight."

She closed her eyes. Her mother had sold her out. She turned to watch him come toward her, his shoes and socks in one hand, his tux pants rolled to midcalf. It was a scene right out of a fantasy. Except Hugh had this little problem with long-term relationships. She told her heart to behave.

Her heart refused. Well, she'd find out what he was up to and then let him know she was heading back to Belcourt Castle. "My mother sent you, didn't she?"

"No. I saw you leave and I followed you."

"I didn't hear anyone behind me."

The moonlight revealed his gentle smile. "I've been in enough suspense flicks to know how to sneak around without getting caught."

"Is there anything you don't know how to do?"

"Yes, and you know exactly what that is."

Oh, God. He was going to apologize for not being the right man for her. She couldn't bear it. "Look, I've accepted the way things are. I even know why, or at least I know enough to have some understanding of the situation. You owe me nothing, not even an explanation. We can part friends, if that's what you're worried about."

He gazed out at the moonlight shimmering on the water. "I have no business being here."

That confused her. "Why not?"

"Never mind." He turned and started back the way he'd come.

"Hugh, what do you mean?"

He swung around and looked at her. "I've let it go to my head—what happened with Gillian, your mom being so nice to me, Harry saying I could do it."

Her heart beat faster. "Do what?"

"Change. Open up. Maybe someday be the kind of man—oh, forget it." He turned away and trudged through the sand.

"No!" She ran after him, sending sand flying in her wake. "I won't forget it." Catching up with him, she grabbed his arm. "Finish that sentence about what kind of man you might be someday."

He gazed down at her. "What if I can't? I won't ask you to be part of some grand experiment. That's not fair."

"Then don't ask me." She tried to get her breath. "I'll just volunteer."

"Kate, I can't let you do that. You're so talented, so full of life, so perfect for some guy without my problems."

She gazed at him, her throat tight. He might not know it, but he'd just told her that he loved her. And because he did, he would sacrifice his own happiness to guarantee hers. She'd been willing to do the same for him.

She swallowed. "We're a pair, you know that? I decided tonight that I couldn't ask you to change to fit my needs, and you've just decided not to ask me to take a chance on you, because you might screw up. Do you know why we're both acting so noble?"

He looked down at her, his expression tender. "I know why I am."

Moisture gathered in her eyes and her voice grew husky. "I know why I am, too."

He took a shaky breath. "I love you, Kate. But the thing is, I've never loved a woman before, so I'm afraid I might really be lousy at it."

"That's okay." She tossed her shoes to the sand. "Because I'm sure that I'll be really good at it."

"I know. And that's why you need to find someone else to—"

"Put down the damned shoes, Hugh."

He dropped them with a soft thud into the sand beside him.

She came in close and ran both hands up the pleats of his white tux shirt. It wasn't very white anymore after his bout with the oak tree. "I love you. You are my hero."

He spanned her waist with his hands in a gesture that could lead to an embrace or not, depending on whether he drew her closer or set her away from him. "I'm not a he—"

"You most certainly are." She wrapped her arms around his neck and held on tight. "Please take me with you to California tomorrow morning."

His jaw dropped. "Take you? So quick? Don't you need to think about it? Plan? Consider?"

"That wouldn't be any fun." Adrenaline pumped through her. So this was what being a risk-taker was like. She'd thought being chronically late added excitement to her life. She'd been settling for chump change. "And it sure wouldn't be very dramatic."

"It's insane. You have your life here. I know you were thinking of making a change, but you should work up to it."

Yesterday he might have talked her out of this decision. But today she was a different person. "Slow and steady's not my style, and it's not yours, either. Bold moves are what keep us alive. You won't have to worry about supporting me or anything. I have savings. But I'm ready to see new country, meet new people, test my talent."

He hesitated. "And what about us?"

"Hugh, I told you. I love you. That means you can take your time deciding how you feel about us. I thought there was no chance that we'd ever be together, but if you think there's any, even a small one, then I'm willing to give it a shot. And I can relocate to California much easier than you can move to Rhode Island."

With a deep sigh, he pulled her in close and gave her a long, soul-shattering kiss. At last he lifted his head to gaze down at her. "I don't need any time to decide how I feel about us. You like bold moves? How about this? Marry me."

A rushing sound filled her ears. "M-marry you?"

He groaned. "No, you don't have to. Forget I said that. We can hang out for a while and you can think about it. We don't—"

"*Yes.*" She clutched him for support because her knees were suddenly like rubber.

"Yes?"

"YES!" It was all coming true—the whirlwind courtship, the dramatic proposal in the moonlight by the most amazing hero she could ever imagine.

He blinked. "You said *yes.*"

"Uh-huh."

His grin flashed. "You said yes!"

She grinned back. "I did."

"Hallelujah!" He picked her up and swung her around until she was dizzy.

"Amen, brother," came a voice from the darkness, followed by a soft chuckle.

Hugh set Kate down and turned. "Harry?"

Smiling broadly, Harry walked toward them with his shoes still on. "May I be the first to congratulate you?"

"You're gonna get lots of sand in your shoes," Hugh said.

"Small matter when my brother's getting married."

"How long have you been there?" Kate asked.

"Not long, but long enough." He clapped Hugh on the shoulder. "Need a best man? I come highly recommended."

Kate watched as the two brothers gazed at each other. Tears filled her eyes as they embraced. Then they ended the gesture with a laugh, as if they were a little embarrassed at being so sentimental.

Harry gave her a brotherly hug. "Thanks for taking a chance on this lug. Now, do you want me to tell everybody to go on back without you? It's a nice night for a walk."

Hugh slipped his arm around Kate's waist. "Yeah, tell them that. You can also tell them that we'll see everybody at breakfast. And don't spread the news yet, okay? I want to do this right. Tomorrow morning I'll ask Kate's dad for her hand in marriage."

Harry nodded. "Nice. Very traditional. I'm sure he'll be impressed. Of course, you could try to impress him even more by coming back with us instead of staying out all night with his daughter."

Hugh pulled Kate closer. "I'm not that interested in impressing him."

Harry laughed. "Didn't think so. See you two in the morning."

As Kate watched him walk away, she said softly, "Hugh, do you think that maybe Harry and Andrea—"

"I'm way ahead of you. Guess who's taking Harry to the airport tomorrow?"

"You're each matchmaking for the other one!"

"Looks like it. And that's really all the time I have for talking about Harry right now. I have something much more important on my mind. There's an interesting little area over there, sort of private looking."

She gazed up at him. "I hate to tell you this, but I didn't bring any—"

"Oh, but I did."

She laughed in surprised delight as he pulled a condom out of his pocket, no doubt the one she'd left at the cottage. "You *planned* this rendezvous?"

"Nope. But I lived in hope."

"That we'd make love one more time before you left?"

"No." He gathered her close, and his lips brushed hers. "That you'd let me love you for the rest of our lives."

HARLEQUIN®
Temptation

THE WRONG BED

What happens when a girl finds herself in the
wrong bed...with the *right* guy?

Find out in:

#866 NAUGHTY BY NATURE by Jule McBride
February 2002

#870 SOMETHING WILD by Toni Blake
March 2002

#874 CARRIED AWAY by Donna Kauffman
April 2002

#878 HER PERFECT STRANGER by Jill Shalvis
May 2002

#882 BARELY MISTAKEN by Jennifer LaBrecque
June 2002

#886 TWO TO TANGLE by Leslie Kelly
July 2002

Midnight mix-ups have never been so much fun!

HARLEQUIN®
Makes any time special®

If you enjoyed what you just read,
then we've got an offer you can't resist!

Take 2 bestselling love stories FREE!

Plus get a FREE surprise gift!

Blaze

The Trueblood, Texas
tradition continues in...

◆ HARLEQUIN® *Blaze* ™

TRULY, MADLY, DEEPLY
by Vicki Lewis Thompson
August 2002

Ten years ago Dustin Ramsey and Erica Mann shared their first
sexual experience. It was a disaster. Now Dustin's determined
to find—and seduce—Erica again, determined to prove to
her, and himself, that he can do better. Much, *much* better.
Only, little does he guess that Erica's got the same agenda....

Don't miss Blaze's next two sizzling Trueblood tales,
written by fan favorites Tori Carrington and Debbi Rawlins.
Available at your nearest bookstore
In September and October 2002.

HARLEQUIN®
Makes any time special ®